W9-BBD-122

Presented to

By

Date

THE Right Choices BIBLE

Dottie and Josh McDowell

Illustrated by Joe Boddy

Tyndale House Publishers, Inc.
Wheaton, Illinois

Visit Tyndale's exciting Web site at www.tyndale.com

Edited by Betty Free
Designed by Beth Sparkman

Library of Congress Cataloging-in-Publication Data

McDowell, Dottie.
The right choices Bible / Dottie and Josh McDowell ; illustrated by Joe Boddy.
p. cm.
Summary: Over sixty stories from the Old and New Testaments, in which the main character must make an important choice.
ISBN 0-8423-3907-8 (hardcover ; alk. paper)
1. Bible stories, English. [1. Bible stories.] I. McDowell, Josh. II. Boddy, Joe, ill. III. Title.
BS551.2.M284 1998
220.9'505—dc21 98-23019

Printed in the United States of America

07 06 05 04 03 02 01 00 99 98
10 9 8 7 6 5 4 3 2 1

Lovingly dedicated

to all our future grandchildren—

whom we can hardly wait to meet!

Josh and Dottie McDowell

ACKNOWLEDGMENTS

We would like to credit the following people for their invaluable contribution to this work:

Cindy Pitts for identifying and rough-drafting many of the Bible stories, which provided insight into how those stories should be presented

Robin Currie for writing the stories, for folding in the Right From Wrong theme of making right choices, and for entering into a child's world to write each story with "childlike energy"

Betty Free of Tyndale House Publishers for her editorial work far beyond the call of duty to tighten, focus, and make each story and application more effective overall

Dave Bellis, our associate for twenty years, for coordinating this project and keeping the content focused and the product orchestrated within the Right From Wrong Campaign

Carla Whitacre Mayer and all of our other friends at Tyndale House Publishers for their high standard of quality and for their commitment to help parents reach their children with the message of God's Word.

CONTENTS

Stories and Choices

CHOICES

What should you eat? And what should you wear?
How should you speak or fix your hair?

You must make choices every day
About many things that come your way.

Yes or no? And large or small?
Give to others or keep it all?

Is it right? Or is it wrong?
You need answers all day long.

God made the world, and God made you.
He knows what's right for you to do!

Bible-time people made choices too.
Their stories can help you know what to do.

Some did wrong with all of their might.
Others pleased God and did what was right.

So read these stories to find your way
Through choices you'll make as you work and play.

(Be sure to look for the grasshoppers, too.
In every story, one's staring at you!)

The First Garden

Genesis 2:4–3:23; 5:4-5

CHOICE: Do Adam and Eve follow God's rule to obey him? Or do they disobey God's rule?

God made a wonderful world with mountains and trees and pumpkins and even a hippopotamus. God also made people to enjoy the wonderful world and take care of it.

The people God made were Adam and Eve. They liked the world God made. It was a garden full of good things like beans and pears and grapes, all ready for them to eat.

But most of all they liked living in the Garden with God. He loved Adam and Eve very much. In fact, he loved them so much that he wanted to help them obey him. So he told them about all the wonderful things they could do. And he warned them about the one thing they should never do. God showed them the tree in the center of the Garden. He said, "Do not eat from that tree. If you eat fruit from that tree, you will die."

God wanted Adam and Eve to obey him. Then he would always keep them safe. They would live in the Garden forever.

A snake lived in the Garden. He was the sneakiest creature of all. He did not love God or the world that God made or the people in it.

One day the snake talked to Eve. He said, "Why don't you eat fruit from the tree in the center of the Garden?"

Eve said, "God told us not to eat from that tree or we will die."

The snake said, "You won't die if you eat it. You'll know everything, just like God does."

Eve saw that the fruit looked very good, and she wanted to taste it.

Now Eve had a big choice to make. She could listen to God and not eat the fruit. Or she could disobey God and eat the fruit.

Eve chose to take some fruit and eat it. She gave some to Adam, and he ate it too. They did not obey

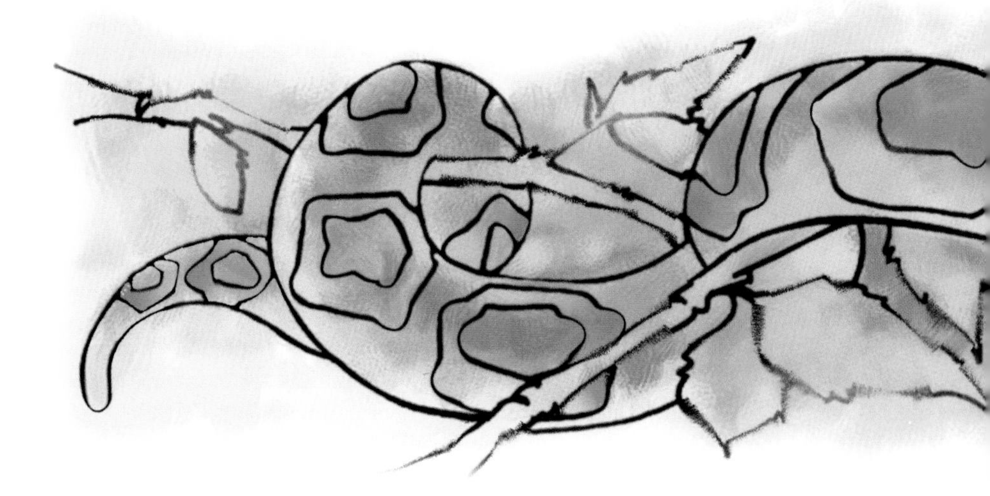

God. So they had to leave the Garden and work hard. They could never go to the Garden again.

After some time, Adam and Eve grew old. Many years later, they died.

God always loved Adam and Eve. But he was very sad. God was sad because Adam and Eve had made the wrong choice and disobeyed him.

Remember Together

Who was the sneakiest creature in the Garden?

What was the one rule God made?

Did Adam and Eve make a good choice or a bad choice?

What sad thing happened to Adam and Eve?

Think about YOUR Choices

Name ways to obey God. (Don't steal or lie; be kind; take care of God's world; follow the rules at my house.) What rules at your house help to keep you safe?

Do a Good-Choice Activity

Draw a sad face and a happy face on two paper circles. Tape a pencil between the circles. At bedtime each night, talk about obeying God. Name times when you didn't obey that day, and hold up the sad face. Then name times when you did obey, and show the happy face.

When we choose to obey, God helps us to be safe and happy!

Pray Together

Dear God, thank you for helping us choose to obey you. Thank you for good rules that keep us safe. In Jesus' name. Amen.

The Floating Zoo

Genesis 6:9–9:17

CHOICE: Does Noah obey God and build an ark? Or does he act like the people around him?

The world God made was getting full of people. Most of them were not kind to each other. They did not obey God. That made God very sad.

But there was a good man named Noah. He and his family loved God and tried to do what was right. They watered their garden and fed their pets. They loved each other, and they were kind to everyone. God was pleased with Noah and his family.

One day God told Noah to build a boat called an ark. God said to make it big and strong, and to fill all the cracks so it would float.

Noah looked all around. He could see his home and a few olive trees and a big desert. But Noah did not see any water to float a big boat in.

God told Noah that he was going to send rain. It would rain and rain and rain. Soon the world would be covered with water. Only Noah and his family would be safe and dry in the boat.

Noah was glad God wanted to take care of his family. But it seemed that a little boat would be just fine. Then God told Noah to gather two of every kind of animal into the boat. That would take a big, big, big boat, for sure!

Noah looked up in the sky, but he didn't see any rain clouds. People would probably laugh if he started to build a boat.

Now Noah had a big choice to make. He could say, "Yes, I'll build the boat. I'll do it even if there is no water and no rain in sight." Or he could say, "No, I won't build the boat. Then my neighbors won't laugh at me."

What did Noah do? He got a hammer and wood, and he began to build the boat. He made it as big as God said to make it. And he filled the cracks so it would float. Then he took two of every kind of animal into the boat. There were tall giraffes and short hedgehogs. There were funny monkeys and fast horses. Finally the slow turtles came. Noah and his family went inside the boat too. God closed the door. Then Noah looked up. It was beginning to rain.

For forty days and nights it rained. The whole earth was covered with water just as God had said. But inside the boat, all of the people and all of the animals were safe and dry.

Finally the rain stopped, and the sun came out. After the earth dried up, it was safe for the people and the animals to leave the boat.

Noah thanked God for keeping him and his family safe. God put a rainbow in the sky. He promised that he would never again cover the whole earth with water.

God always loved Noah and was glad he had made a good choice.

Remember Together

Why was God pleased with only Noah and his family?

What was Noah's choice?

Did Noah make a good choice or a bad choice?

What did God put in the sky as a promise to never send so much water again?

Think about YOUR Choices

God gives you a family to keep you safe and dry. What do they tell you to put on when it's raining? Your friends may not have the same rules to stay safe that your family has. Will you obey your rules anyway?

Do a Good-Choice Activity

Gather all your stuffed animals and pretend you are Noah. Your bed can be the boat. As Noah, will you be like the people who don't please God, or will you obey God?

Obeying God might mean that we don't do what everyone else is doing.

Pray Together

Dear God, we're glad that we can choose to obey you even when others don't. Thank you for keeping us safe from thunder and lightning. In Jesus' name. Amen.

Build It Bigger!

Genesis 11:1-9

CHOICE: Do the people accept that God is in charge? Or do they try to become powerful like him?

There was a time when many people liked to make a lot of bricks to build things. Bricks in the morning. Bricks at noon. Bricks at dinnertime. All day long they made bricks.

The people could make a lot of bricks because everyone could understand everyone else. All of the people called things by the same names. Someone who needed more mud for the bricks just said "mud."

Everyone knew what he wanted and brought him mud. Someone who needed water just said "water." Everyone knew what she wanted and brought her water. Someone who needed straw just said "straw." Everyone knew what he wanted and brought him straw.

All day and all night people worked hard making bricks. Why? Because they thought they were building

something wonderful. They were building a city with a tower. The tower would be strong and tall. It would reach all the way to heaven. The people thought that if they built that tower to heaven, they could climb it. Then they would be as powerful as God.

But God was not pleased. He knew that the people were not wise enough to be so powerful. They would make mistakes and hurt others.

Now the people had a big choice to make. Should

they keep building their tower and try to be as powerful as God? Or should they stop building and remember that God is in charge?

The people kept building the tower, higher and higher.

God was not happy. So he gave the people different languages. Now when one person said "mud," some people brought him straw. Others brought him water. No one could understand anyone else. The people could not make any more bricks.

The city and the tower that the people had tried to build were called Babel. That's because the words people said got mixed up there. All people no longer said the same kinds of words.

People began to move away and start building many different cities. In each city everyone spoke the same kinds of words. Before long, the city of Babel was empty. And the Tower of Babel was just a pile of broken bricks.

God loved the people of Babel. He was sorry they chose to think they could be as powerful as he is.

Remember Together

Why were the people building a tower?
Did the people of Babel make a good choice or a bad choice?
What did God do to stop the people from building?
Where did the people go to live?

Think about YOUR Choices

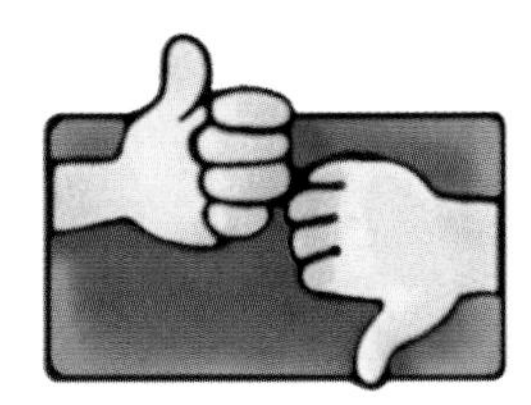

At home, who is in charge? At school, who is in charge? What are some things that happen when we choose not to obey the person in charge?

Do a Good-Choice Activity

Take care of your stuffed animals (or live pets). Then give them something to do. How do you feel if they obey you? How do you feel if they don't? (With stuffed animals, pretend that they obey or don't obey.)

God is in charge of everyone, and he knows what's best for everyone!

Pray Together

Dear God, help me choose to let you be in charge all the time. In Jesus' name. Amen.

Leaving Home

Genesis 12:1-8; 13:2

CHOICE: Does Abraham obey God's direction to move far away? Or does he stay where he is?

Abraham lived in a tent. He lived there with his wife, Sarah. Outside the tent they could cook their food over a big fire. And they could rest under a shade tree. Abraham's goats and sheep ate green grass in the fields. The cattle drank water at the well. Abraham was very happy with his tent home.

Sometimes Abraham moved to another field close by. He moved when there was no green grass left. He moved when the well went dry. He and Sarah would pack their things. They would take all of their helpers and all of their animals. They would move to a new place and set up their tent.

One day God told Abraham to move far away. He wanted Abraham to have a place to stay forever. He wanted Abraham to have a family. Abraham's family would love and praise God as their only God. "Leave this place and go to a place I will show you," said God. "I will take care of you there. It can be your family's home forever."

Abraham looked at his nice tent and his animals. They had plenty of grass and water where they were. It would be a lot of trouble to move everyone.

Now Abraham had a big choice to make. He could obey God and pack up his things. He could move to wherever God led him. Or he could stay comfortable living in his tent by the well and the big tree.

This is what Abraham did. He packed all his things so he could follow God. He and Sarah folded all their clothes and put them on donkeys. Then they packed food on camels. Abraham rounded up the sheep and the goats. He gave the cattle one last drink of water. Then he took down his tent and put out his cooking fire. He left his place by the shade tree.

Abraham was moving to wherever God led him. He knew he would not be coming back.

Abraham traveled for a long time. His wife, Sarah, was with him. His brother's son, Lot, was with him too. Finally they came to a new land, a place they had never seen before. There was plenty of green grass for the sheep and goats to eat. And there was plenty of water for the cows to drink. There was a place to put up the tent and a shade tree to sit under.

Abraham and Sarah and Lot were happy in their new home. They praised God and became his special people.

God was happy that Abraham moved to the new land. God blessed Abraham and gave him everything he needed—and more!

Remember Together

Did Abraham like his home in the tent?
What did God want Abraham to do?
Did Abraham make a good choice or a bad choice?
What did God do for Abraham?

Think about YOUR Choices

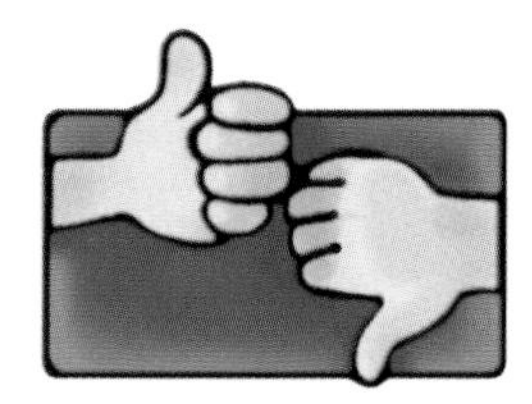

How can you know if God wants you to move or stay where you are? If your family had to move, what would you pack? God always goes with you, just like he went with Abraham!

Do a Good-Choice Activity

Share stories of moves the family has made. Or talk about how it feels when friends move away. Look at pictures of former homes and identify objects that were packed with care. How did God take care of you?

God helps us choose to go where he leads.

Pray Together

Dear God, we're glad you are always with us, even if we move. Help us choose to follow you wherever you lead us. In Jesus' name. Amen.

Sharing the Land

Genesis 13:5-18

CHOICE: Does Abraham let Lot choose the land he wants? Or does Abraham take the best land?

Abraham loved God. He followed God to a new land. It was a land with grass and streams of water. Abraham needed the grass and water for his animals. He had a lot of sheep and goats. He had a lot of cows, too.

Lot had sheep and goats and cows, just like his uncle did. He needed grass and water for his animals too.

Abraham and Lot both had helpers. The helpers took care of the animals. Abraham's helpers and Lot's helpers began to fight. Abraham's helpers wanted the grass and water for Abraham's animals. Lot's helpers wanted the grass and water for Lot's animals.

Abraham looked out over the land. God had said the land would belong to his family forever.

Now Abraham had a big choice to make. He could let his nephew have part of the land. Why, he could even let Lot choose which part he wanted! Or he could tell Lot to get off his land. He could keep it all for himself.

Abraham knew that God wanted the land to belong to his whole family. God wanted them to be his

special people. He wanted them to praise him, not fight over the land. Abraham said to Lot, "There is plenty of land. You may choose the part you want."

So Lot picked the land with the most green grass. He picked the land with the best streams of water.

Lot moved away. Then Abraham looked out on his land again. God said to him, "I will give you a very big family. This land will always belong to them."

Then Abraham went to a place where there were some big trees. He praised God there. He was glad that God would always take care of his family.

Remember Together

Who came to the new land with Abraham?
Why did Lot need some land for himself?
Did Abraham make a good choice or a bad choice?
What did Abraham do after Lot went away?

Think about YOUR Choices

What things do you have that God might want you to share with someone? Be sure to take some time every day to praise God and thank him for all his gifts.

Do a Good-Choice Activity

Retell the Bible story, making animal sounds for the sheep and goats and cows. Be sure to cheer when Abraham makes his good choice!

God is glad when we share the gifts he gives us, just like Abraham did.

Pray Together

Dear God, help us choose to share the gifts you give us. We want to do our part to see that people have what they need. In Jesus' name. Amen.

Sarah's Baby

Genesis 18:1-15; 21:1-7

CHOICE: Does Sarah trust God to keep his promise? Or does she think it is impossible?

Sarah was married to Abraham. She lived in a nice tent, and she liked to cook over the big fire. Every night she looked up at the stars in the sky.

But Sarah wanted something she did not have. Sarah wanted a baby. She wanted to hold and cuddle a baby, rock it to sleep, and teach the baby all about God's wonderful world.

God had promised Abraham that he would have a son. But every year his wife, Sarah, got older and older. She was old enough to be a grandmother or even a great-grandmother. But she still did not have a baby.

God wanted Abraham and Sarah to know that he had

not forgotten his promise. He was going to give them a child. So God sent three men to visit Abraham. They were really angels. One of them, God's angel, said to Abraham, "This time next year, Sarah will have her baby."

Sarah was listening from inside the tent. She giggled to herself. She thought, *I can't have a baby now. I'm too old.*

God's angel said to Abraham, "Nothing is impossible for God. Next year Sarah will have a baby."

Now Sarah had a big choice to make. She could believe God and wait a little longer for a baby. Or she could think it was impossible for God to give her a baby.

What did Sarah do? She waited a little while longer for God's promise. And a year later, when Sarah was almost 100 years old, she did have a baby. She named him Isaac, which means "laughter." Isaac made Abraham and Sarah laugh. He was a special gift from God. Now they had a son to live on the land after them.

God can do things that seem impossible. Sarah made a good choice to trust God and wait for him to send her a baby.

Remember Together

What promise did God want Abraham and Sarah to remember?

Why might it have been hard for Sarah to believe God?

Did Sarah make a good choice or a bad choice?

What did she name the new baby?

Think about YOUR Choices

What promises have people made to you? Do you believe they will keep their promises? Why or why not? God promises to love you and take care of you. Can you believe him? Why or why not?

Do a Good-Choice Activity

Name some ways God has kept his promise to love you and take care of you. Draw a picture of yourself to show how this makes you feel.

Choosing to believe God's promises always brings happiness.

Pray Together

Dear God, give us patience when we have to wait for promises to be kept. Help us choose to believe all your promises. In Jesus' name. Amen.

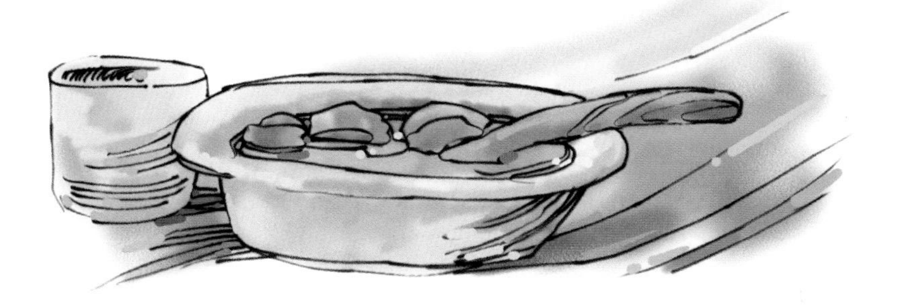

The Bowl of Stew

Genesis 25:19-34

CHOICE: Does Esau choose to lead his family someday? Or does he just think about what he needs right now?

Abraham and Sarah's son, baby Isaac, grew up. He married Rebekah. Isaac became the father of two sons, both born on the same day. The boys were twins, but they did not look alike or act alike.

One son was covered with a lot of hair when he was born. His name was Esau. He was born just a few minutes earlier than his brother. So he was the older son. Someday it would be his job to be the leader of

his family. When Esau grew up, he was strong and lived outdoors.

Isaac's other son was holding on to his brother's foot when he was born. His name was Jacob. When Jacob grew up, he always stayed near his home. He liked to cook the meat and fish that Esau brought home. Then the brothers would eat the food together. Jacob was the younger son, but only by a

few minutes. Jacob wanted to be the leader of the family.

One day Esau came in from hunting and was very hungry. Jacob had been cooking all day. He had a big pot of stew cooking over the fire. Mmmm. It smelled so good. The smell was all over the camp. Esau smelled it and felt very, very hungry. He was ready to give Jacob anything for a bowl of that stew.

Jacob decided to trick Esau. He said to Esau, "I'll let you eat some stew. But you must let me have your place in the family. Will you let me be the leader of our family someday?"

Now Esau had a big choice to make. He could wait to find something else to eat. Then he could still be the leader of his family someday. Or he could eat the stew right away. Then he would have to give his place in the family to Jacob.

Esau was really hungry. So he said, "It is yours. You can be the leader of our family someday. But give me that stew."

Jacob gave him the stew. Esau was so hungry that he ate and ate and ate. He didn't even think about what he had done. He had traded his place in the family for a bowl of stew.

God was sorry that Esau had been so impatient and foolish. But God would help Esau's brother, Jacob, be a wise family leader.

Remember Together

What did Jacob want from Esau?
Why did Esau give up his place in the family?
Did Esau make a good choice or a bad choice?

Think about YOUR Choices

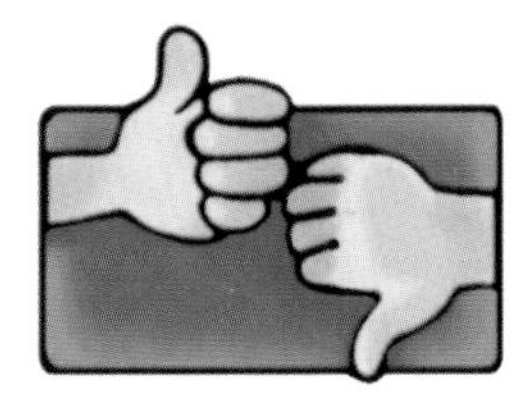

Did you ever feel as if you just had to do something? Maybe you ate a whole box of candy. Or you played with a friend instead of going home as you were told. What happened?

Do a Good-Choice Activity

Decide which would be right to do; then do one of those things: Help your mom or yell at her. Eat dinner or skip dinner and watch TV. Plan to read a Bible story every day or never make such plans.

The things we choose to do today may change what happens tomorrow.

Pray Together

Dear God, help us take time to do what is important. Help us remember that choosing to love and serve you is most important of all. In Jesus' name. Amen.

Hairy Arms

Genesis 27

CHOICE: Does Jacob tell the truth? Or does he lie to his father?

Jacob wanted to be the leader of his family. He had tricked Esau into giving up his right to be the family leader. But Jacob needed something else. He needed his father's blessing. His father, Isaac, was very old now. He couldn't hear very well, and he couldn't see at all.

Jacob's mother said, "I have an idea. Your brother, Esau, has hairy arms. Tie these goatskins onto your arms and pretend to be him. Then your father, Isaac, will give you his blessing."

Jacob wanted to be the family leader, so he agreed. He put the goatskins on his arms and went to Isaac's tent. He brought some goat meat that his mother had cooked.

Isaac smelled the good dinner. He thought it was wild meat that Esau had brought home. Jacob let him think that. Isaac ate it all up. Then Isaac said, "The blessing goes to my oldest son, Esau. Esau has hairy arms. Do you have hairy arms? Are you Esau?"

Now Jacob had a big choice to make. He could tell the truth. Then his father would not give him the blessing that was meant for Esau. Or Jacob could lie. He could say he was Esau and get his father's special blessing. Then he would become the family leader.

What did Jacob do? Jacob let his father feel his hairy arms. Isaac could not see the son, but he believed it was Esau. So he gave the boy his blessing.

Jacob was now the family leader. When Esau found

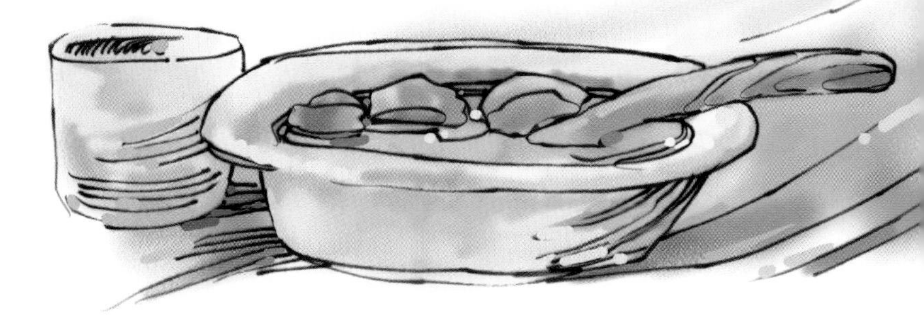

out, he was angry. He was so angry that he made plans to hurt Jacob if he found him.

Jacob's mother helped him pack his things. Jacob was the family leader, but for now he couldn't stay with his family. He had to run far away from Esau.

God was sorry that Jacob told a lie. But God still loved Jacob and traveled with him wherever he went.

Remember Together

How did Jacob lie to his father?
What happened to Jacob because of his bad choice?

Think about YOUR Choices

What is the difference between a lie, a little white lie, a tall tale, and an exaggerated story? Can you think of times when it's hard for you to tell the truth? What happens when you tell a lie—a little white one or a big tall tale?

Do a Good-Choice Activity

Use blocks to build a long road for Jacob to escape from Esau. Pretend to be Jacob and tell how you feel as you get farther and farther away from your family.

Telling the truth is always better than telling a lie.

Pray Together

Dear God, we're sorry about the times we have told a lie. Thank you for forgiving us and loving us. In Jesus' name. Amen.

Brothers

Genesis 32–33

CHOICE: Does Esau forgive Jacob? Or does he stay angry?

Jacob was lonely. He had been away from home for a long, long time. He had been gone so long that he had a big family of his own. He had lots of goats and camels and sheep. He had lots of cows and donkeys, too. But he was lonely. He missed his brother, Esau.

Jacob wanted to go home, but he was afraid. Esau had been really angry when he left. Maybe he would still try to hurt Jacob. Maybe he would try to hurt Jacob's family, too.

Jacob was so lonely that he finally decided to go home anyway. He would trust God to make things right between him and Esau.

So he packed up his family and his animals. And he started home.

Jacob sent a message to Esau. He let Esau know that he was coming home. Then Jacob heard that Esau was coming to meet him. And he had 400 men with him!

Jacob was afraid. He talked to God. He said, "You told me to go back to my family. You promised to be

kind to me. You've loved me, and you've taken good care of me. I have a big family. Now I need your help. Please keep me safe from Esau."

The next day Jacob sent a lot of animals as a present to Esau. He sent goats and sheep and camels. He sent cows and donkeys, too.

The day after that, Jacob saw Esau and his 400 men

coming. Messengers had brought Esau the gift of animals and the news: It is your brother, Jacob.

Jacob! After all these years. Jacob had tricked him out of being the family leader. And now Jacob was coming home.

Esau had a big choice to make. He could send his 400 men to hurt Jacob and his family. Or he could forgive Jacob. And he could admit that he had made a bad choice. He should not have traded his place in the family for a bowl of stew.

Esau rounded up his family, his animals, and his soldiers. He started to march out toward Jacob. Jacob saw the big crowd. He saw Esau in front. Jacob was afraid, but he did not turn back. He told his family to stop, and he went on alone. He walked slowly toward Esau, greeting his brother in a kind, friendly way.

Esau held out his arms and hugged Jacob. Both brothers laughed and talked and cheered all at once. It was so good to be together again! They knew that God wanted them to be together and live in peace.

God had traveled with Jacob. Now he brought Jacob safely home to be the family leader.

Remember Together

Why was Jacob afraid to go home to Esau?
What did Esau do when he saw Jacob?
Did Esau make a good choice or a bad choice?
Were the brothers glad to be back together?
How do you know?

Think about YOUR Choices

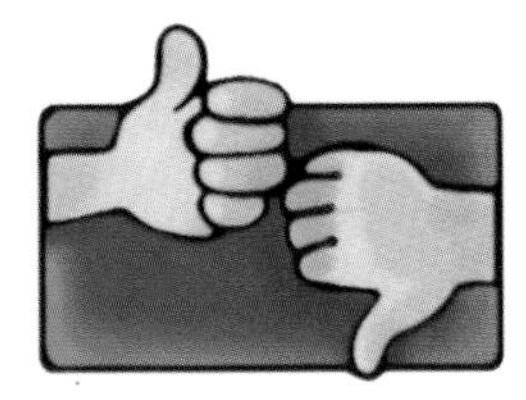

Remember times in your family when someone had to forgive another member of the family. Was it easy? hard? What feelings did everyone have before and after the forgiveness took place?

Do a Good-Choice Activity

On a small paper plate draw an ugly little creature. That can be the family "Grudge." When someone is angry, give that person the Grudge to hold on to. Most likely, that family member won't stay angry! See how much better it feels to choose to forgive and let the Grudge go.

Forgiveness is better than holding on to an ugly grudge.

Pray Together

Dear God, help us choose to forgive others even when they hurt us or trick us. In Jesus' name. Amen.

Into the Pit

Genesis 37:12-35

CHOICE: Are Joseph's brothers kind to him? Or do they send him away?

Jacob had twelve sons. Sometimes they all worked together. And sometimes they had fights, just like all brothers do.

One son was named Joseph. Joseph was the youngest of all the brothers. He spent a lot of time with his father, Jacob. The older brothers worked in the fields and watched the sheep. Now Joseph was a teenager, and he helped take care of the sheep too.

Sometimes Jacob gave special gifts to one son, sometimes to another, just like all fathers do. But one day he gave Joseph something very special—a wonderful new coat. Joseph's brothers all had coats too. Some were gray or green or brown. But Joseph's coat had every color of the rainbow in it. It had yellow and red and blue. It had purple and gold and silver. It was a wonderful coat. Joseph put it right on. How happy he was! But the brothers were jealous of Joseph's beautiful new coat.

One night Joseph had a strange dream. When he woke up, he told his brothers all about it. He said, "I dreamed you were eleven bundles of wheat. I was the twelfth bundle. All of you had to bow down to me because I was the most important."

Joseph's brothers didn't want to bow down to their little brother. They didn't want to hear about any more of his dreams. So they were very upset when Joseph told them about another dream. This time the sun and moon and eleven stars bowed down to Joseph. His father asked, "Will your mother and I bow down to you someday? Will your eleven brothers all bow down to you?"

Joseph's brothers were so jealous. They remembered that their father, Jacob, had given a special gift to their little brother. And now Joseph was saying that they would have to bow down to him too?

The brothers had a big choice to make. They could leave Joseph alone and go back to work. And they could remember the nice presents they may have gotten from their father. Or they could take the coat away from Joseph. And they could hurt him so he wouldn't be in their way anymore.

What did they do? All those big brothers ganged up on Joseph. They did it when Joseph came to the field to see if they were OK. His father had sent him.

The brothers were OK, but soon Joseph was not OK. His brothers took his fine coat from him and put him in a big pit. They were going to kill him. Then they saw some traders from Egypt.

One brother had an idea. He said, "Let's sell Joseph to the traders who are going to Egypt."

So they did.

Then they took the wonderful new coat and got it dirty. They made it look as if Joseph had been fighting with an animal. They took the coat to Jacob and let him think that Joseph had been killed by a wild animal.

Jacob was very, very sad. He thought that he would never see Joseph again.

God was very sad that the brothers were so unkind to Joseph. But God traveled with Joseph to Egypt and was with him always.

Remember Together

How did Joseph's brothers feel about his new coat?

How did Joseph's dreams make his brothers feel?

What did Joseph's brothers do to him?

Did the brothers make a good choice or a bad choice?

Think about YOUR Choices

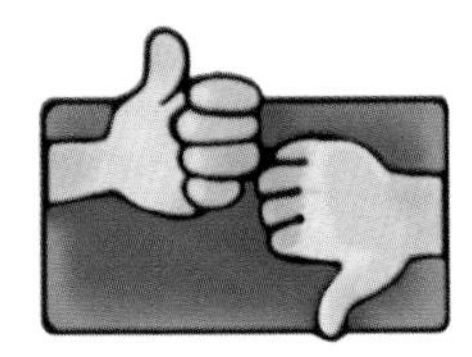

What kinds of things make you feel jealous of a brother? a sister? a friend? What can you do with those feelings so they will not be hurtful?

Do a Good-Choice Activity

Color a paper with all the colors Joseph's coat may have had. As you color, think of something kind to do. Then do it for a person who has something you'd like to have.

God wants us to be happy about what we have and what others have.

Pray Together

Dear God, help us to be kind to others. Help us to be happy for them even if they have something we'd like to have. In Jesus' name. Amen.

A Long Wait

Genesis 39; 41

CHOICE: Does Joseph trust God to work things out in God's own time? Or does Joseph question God's plan?

Joseph was far away from home. The traders who had bought him took him to Egypt. There he had to work for a rich man. Joseph was a good worker and did everything he should. But the rich man's wife became angry with Joseph. She tricked her husband into putting Joseph in prison.

Joseph could not see the birds or feel the rain on his face. He did not like being in prison at all. Day after day he hoped that God would help him get out of prison. But day after day nothing happened.

Now Joseph had a big choice to make. He could give up waiting for God's help and try to get out on his own.

Maybe he could talk one of the guards into letting him go. Maybe he could steal the keys and escape. Or he could trust God. He could believe that everything that had happened to him was part of God's plan. And he could wait for God to show him what to do.

Joseph decided to trust God. He still did not get out of prison for a long time. But one day a man came to see Joseph. This man was a helper for the pharaoh himself.

The pharaoh was like a king over all of Egypt. He had heard that Joseph could tell the meaning of dreams. The pharaoh had dreamed a special dream. He wanted Joseph to tell him what that special dream meant.

Joseph went with the pharaoh's helper and listened as Pharaoh told his dream. It was about seven fat cows and seven thin cows.

God showed Joseph what the dream meant. Joseph

said, "The seven fat cows mean that there will be seven good years. Grain crops will grow, and there will be lots of food. The seven thin cows mean that there will be seven bad years. Grain crops won't grow, and there will be no food at all."

Pharaoh asked, "What shall we do?"

Joseph said, "While there is a lot of grain, store it in big bins. Then the extra grain can be used to make food when there isn't enough."

Joseph became an important helper for the pharaoh. He was put in charge of all the grain crops in the country. When there was a lot of grain, he put some in big bins and saved it.

Then for seven years there was no rain, and all the crops died. There was no food anywhere. But Joseph had grain in the bins. He gave some to each person. Then everyone could use the grain to make food.

God was glad Joseph trusted him and waited for his help. God had a good plan for Joseph. He helped Joseph become an important leader in Egypt.

Remember Together

How did Joseph feel when he was in prison?

Why would trying to get out of prison on his own have been a bad choice?

How did Joseph help the pharaoh—and everyone else?

Think about YOUR Choices

Have you ever waited a long time for God to answer a prayer? Maybe you're waiting for an answer now. Can you be like Joseph? Can you wait and trust God?

Do a Good-Choice Activity

Act out doing different kinds of jobs. Someday you'll grow up. And God will help you know what he wants you to do.

Waiting for God's answer is always a good thing to do.

Pray Together

Dear God, thank you that you answer our prayers at just the right time. Thank you for your plans for each of us. Be with us as we wait to find out what you want us to do. In Jesus' name. Amen.

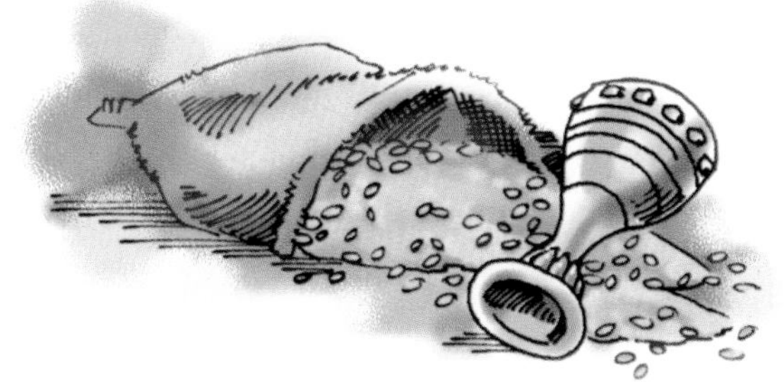

"I Am Joseph!"

Genesis 42–45

CHOICE: Does Joseph think about the good things that happen? Or does he just think about the bad things?

After Joseph's brothers had sold him to traders from Egypt, they had gone back to their father, Jacob. They had let their father think that Joseph was dead.

The brothers knew that Joseph was alive. But they thought they would never see him again.

One year no grain crops would grow. The next year no crops would grow again. The third year the same thing happened. This went on for seven years. Finally there was no grain left to make food. That was the bad news.

But then Jacob heard some good news: There was

grain in Egypt! A smart man in Egypt had saved a lot of grain in bins.

Jacob called his sons to him. He told them to go to Egypt and buy some grain. Then they could make food, and they would not have to starve.

The brothers got on camels and left right away.

They traveled for a long time and finally got to Egypt. There they asked for the important man who had saved a lot of grain. When they got to see the man, they were very polite. They bowed low and asked to buy some grain. They didn't know that this man was their brother Joseph.

But Joseph knew that the men were his brothers. He knew that long ago they had sold him to a trader from Egypt. He also knew that there was a younger brother named Benjamin still at home. So Joseph kept one of the older brothers in Egypt. He sent the other brothers back home to get Benjamin. He sent sacks of grain with them and put their money back in the sacks.

The brothers didn't know what to think. They were afraid of what Joseph would do to them. But finally they went back to Egypt with Benjamin. Joseph asked all of them to eat at his house.

Soon the brothers started back home again with more sacks of grain. But Joseph had tricked them and had hidden his special silver cup in Benjamin's sack. Joseph sent out a helper to bring the men back to Egypt once again. He told them he would have to keep Benjamin in Egypt for stealing his silver cup. But the older brothers said they couldn't let him do that. Their father would be too sad. So Joseph knew that his older brothers had learned to be kind.

Now Joseph had a big choice to make. He could think about the good things that had happened

because he was living in Egypt. He could think about the grain he had saved. And he could think about the people who were able to make food with the grain. Then he could tell his brothers who he was. He could forgive them for all they had done. Or he could remember only the bad things that his brothers had done. He could throw his brothers into prison to get back at them.

This is what Joseph did. He said, “I am Joseph! I am your brother.”

The brothers were afraid. But Joseph said, "I know you wanted to hurt me. But God let me come to Egypt so I could help my family. There is plenty of grain here to make food. Bring my father to Egypt, and we will all be together again."

Joseph knew that it was God who had brought good from bad in his life. God was glad that Joseph knew this. God was also glad that Joseph forgave his brothers and helped his family.

Remember Together

Why did Joseph's brothers go to Egypt?

What bad thing did Joseph remember when he saw his brothers?

Did Joseph think only about the bad thing his brothers did?

Did Joseph make a good choice or a bad choice?

What good did God bring out of the bad in Joseph's life?

Think about YOUR Choices

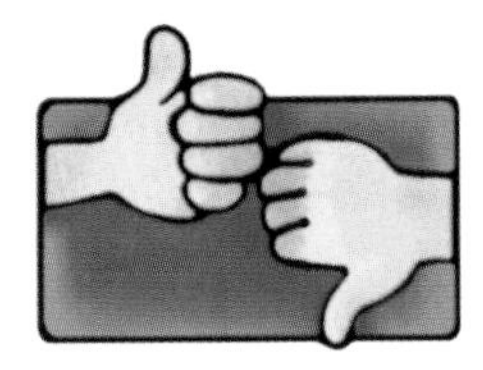

When has a bad situation turned out good in your family? How do you feel when you think only about what's bad? How do you feel when you find the good that comes out of the bad?

Do a Good-Choice Activity

Make up a story about some bad news. Then make up a happy ending for the story.

Even when bad things happen, we can believe that God has good plans for us.

Pray Together

Dear God, give us courage when bad things happen. Help us to believe that you can bring good out of the bad. In Jesus' name. Amen.

The Floating Basket

Exodus 1:6–2:10

CHOICE: Does Miriam help her baby brother? Or does she run away?

Many years after Joseph and his brothers lived in Egypt, there was a new pharaoh. He did not like God's people. He made them work as slaves to build great buildings that would honor him. They had to work very hard. They made bricks and carried water and moved big stones.

Pharaoh was afraid that God's people would fight against him. So he came up with an evil plan. It was a plan to keep the number of God's people from getting any larger. Pharaoh said that God's people could not have any baby boys.

One mother had a new baby boy, and she loved him very much. She came up with her own plan. It was a good plan. The mother hid her baby for three months. Then she began weaving a strong basket. She put mud in all the cracks so that the basket was waterproof. She also put soft cloth in the basket. That made a nice little bed to hide her baby boy in.

The baby's mother took the basket and the baby to the Nile River. The baby's big sister, Miriam, went with them.

The mother kissed her baby and put him in the basket. Then she carefully set it in the water. It floated! Her little boy did not get wet at all. Then Mother had to go home.

Miriam stayed to watch the basket with her baby brother in it. Soon she heard voices. Miriam peeked through the tall grass and saw the pharaoh's daughter! The princess had come down to the river to take a bath. Maybe she would see the basket and find the baby. What would Miriam do?

Now Miriam had a big choice to make. She could stay and try to help her little brother. Or she could run away.

This is what Miriam did. She stayed to watch and listen. Pharaoh's daughter saw the basket and called for one of her helpers to get it. As soon as the princess saw

the baby inside, she loved him. She named him Moses. And she said that Moses would be like her own son.

Miriam still didn't run away. Instead, she ran right up to the princess. She said, "I can find someone to take care of the baby for you. Would you like me to do that?"

"Oh, yes. That would be very helpful," said the princess.

Miriam ran home to tell her mother the wonderful news: They could take care of baby Moses for the princess! And the baby would be safe. Someday he would live in the pharaoh's house!

God was glad that Miriam helped her family. Miriam helped to keep little Moses safe. And that was all part of God's plan!

Remember Together

Why did a mother make a boat for her baby boy?

How did the baby's big sister, Miriam, help him?

Did Miriam make a good choice or a bad choice?

Think about YOUR Choices

What are some ways that you help in your family? Are there times when you would like to run away instead of help? What should you do then?

Do a Good-Choice Activity

Float a large leaf in some water to see how Moses' basket floated in the water. Then work with your family to make a list of water safety rules. You can help everyone remember to obey the rules!

We can ask God to show us how to be good helpers.

Pray Together

Dear God, we want to do what we can to be helpful. Show us how to help our families each day. In Jesus' name. Amen.

"Not Me!"

Exodus 2:11–4:20

CHOICE: Does Moses listen to God? Or doesn't he care about what God says?

Moses grew up like a prince in Egypt. He was like a grandson of the pharaoh. But Moses knew that he was really one of God's people.

One day Moses looked at all the hard work that God's people were doing. These were his people, and he was angry that they were slaves. He tried to help them, but he was too upset. The way he tried to help did not please God. And Moses made the pharaoh angry too.

So Moses ran away from Egypt. He worked as a shepherd, taking care of sheep for many years.

One day as Moses was watching the sheep, he saw a strange sight. It looked like a bush was burning. But the fire did not seem to destroy the bush. He walked closer. Then he heard the voice of God. Moses took off his sandals because he was standing in a very special place.

God wanted Moses to go back to Egypt. God said, "I want you to take my people out of Egypt. Take them to their own land." Would Moses do it?

Moses said, "Not me! How can I tell Pharaoh to let the people go?"

God said, "I will be with you every minute." Would Moses do it?

Moses said, "Not me! Your people won't believe me. They will want to know your name. Then what will I tell them?"

God said to Moses, "You can call me 'I am.' That is my name." Would Moses do it?

Moses said, "Not me! The people will say I never saw you."

Then God told Moses to put his shepherd's stick down on the ground. When he did, the stick became a snake! God told Moses to take hold of the snake's tail. He did, and it became a stick again. "Do this for the people," said God. "Then they will know that you have seen me." Would Moses do it?

Moses said, "Not me! I don't speak very well."

God said that he would help Moses speak. But finally God said that Moses' brother, Aaron, could go too. Aaron was a good speaker.

Now Moses had a big choice to make. He had been listening to God, so he knew what God wanted him to do. He could go to Egypt as God had asked. Or he could keep arguing with God and not do what God wanted.

Moses chose to do what God wanted. He agreed at last to go back to Egypt.

God rejoiced that Moses had listened to him. Moses had thought he couldn't do what God asked. But Moses cared about what God said. And Moses was going to help save God's people.

Remember Together

What did God want Moses to do?
What were some of Moses' excuses?
Did Moses make a good choice or a bad choice?

Think about YOUR Choices

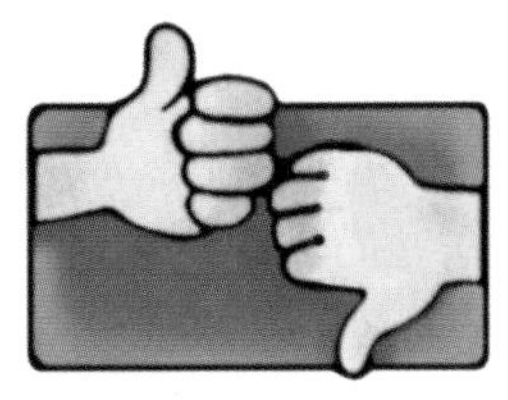

Can you think of any places where you don't like to go? Tell God how you feel. Then ask him to help you just as he helped Moses.

Do a Good-Choice Activity

Next time you are in the car, think about God's being with you. At each stop you can say, "God is with us here at the (bank, library, store, etc.)."

God helps us do the things he asks us to do.

Pray Together

Dear God, sometimes you ask us to do hard things. Give us courage to choose to do them. And give us faith to know that you are there with us through everything. In Jesus' name. Amen.

"NO!"

Exodus 7–10

CHOICE: Does Pharaoh believe in God's power? Or doesn't he believe in God's power?

Moses went back to Egypt with his brother, Aaron. They told Pharaoh that God wanted his people to be set free. Pharaoh didn't believe them. So Aaron threw down his shepherd's stick. It became a snake.

But the pharaoh still wouldn't believe, and he wouldn't let the people go. Pharaoh said, "No!"

Moses told Pharaoh that his God, the one true God, was more powerful than all the gods Pharaoh had.

Pharaoh thought about his many gods. Why should he obey this one God of Moses? Pharaoh said, "No!"

So God made bad things happen to the people of Egypt. These bad things were called plagues. God sent

rivers of blood and dead frogs. Moses asked Pharaoh again, "Now will you let God's people go?

But Pharaoh said, "No!"

So God sent little biting flies and big flies. He sent a sickness that killed animals. Another sickness covered both animals and people with sores on their skin. Then God sent hail and locusts and darkness. The people of Egypt were really scared.

"Now will you let God's people go?" Moses asked.

Now Pharaoh had a big choice to make. He could believe in God's power. He could admit that God had power over the weather and the rivers and the animals and the people. And he could let God's people go. Or he could keep God's people as his slaves.

Once more Pharaoh said, "No!"

God was very unhappy that Pharaoh did not believe in his power. God had sent Moses to free his people, and someday soon God would help him do it.

Remember Together

What did God want Pharaoh to do?

Can you name one or more of the plagues God sent?

Did Pharaoh make a good choice or a bad choice?

Think about YOUR Choices

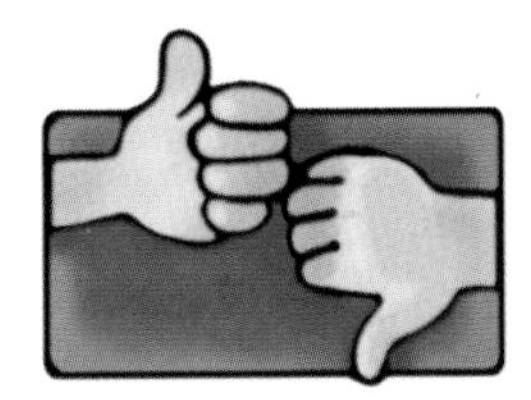

Will you choose to believe that God is powerful? Remember that he wants to use his power to help you. Name a way that he can help you when you are sick . . . hurt . . . in a storm . . . sad.

Do a Good-Choice Activity

Make a list of things that nature can harm us with: lightning, blizzards, earthquakes, etc. How good to know that God is with us in all these things! He is with us just as he was with his people in Egypt.

We can believe that God is powerful and that he loves us too!

Pray Together

Dear God, help us to believe in you and in your power. You love us, and we love you. In Jesus' name. Amen.

The Passover Meal

Exodus 11–12

CHOICE: Do God's people trust him to save them? Or do they think that God can't get them out of Egypt?

Pharaoh would not let God's people leave Egypt. So God made many bad things happen in Egypt. But when Moses asked Pharaoh to let God's people go, he still said, "No."

God got ready to send the Angel of Death to Egypt. But first God wanted to make sure that all of his people would be safe. He gave Moses careful directions. Then Moses told the people what to do. "Paint lamb's blood around your doors. This will show the Angel of Death that he is to pass over your houses. Make bread without yeast so you can make it quickly. Then eat a lamb dinner, and be ready to leave in a hurry.

Now God's people had a big choice to make. They

could obey God and be ready, painting their doors and eating quickly as he commanded. Or they could go on with life as usual.

This is what God's people did. They painted lamb's blood around their doors. The Angel of Death was in their town.

They made bread with no yeast in it because there was no time to let it rise. They ate the bread with bitter herbs to remind them of the sad times they had as slaves. The Angel of Death was on their street.

They ate with their cloaks on so they could leave in a hurry. The Angel of Death was on their block.

Now the lamb's blood around their doors protected them. The Angel of Death passed over the houses of God's people. Not one of God's people died.

The Angel of Death did go to Pharaoh's house. He went to all of the houses of the people of Egypt.

During the night, Pharaoh called Moses and Aaron to come to him. This time Pharaoh said, "Go!"

God's people were free!

God was glad that his people trusted and obeyed him. God kept them safe. God set them free.

Remember Together

How did God save his people from the Angel of Death?

Did the people trust God and obey him?

Did God's people make a good choice or a bad choice?

What did Pharaoh say to Moses that night?

Think about YOUR Choices

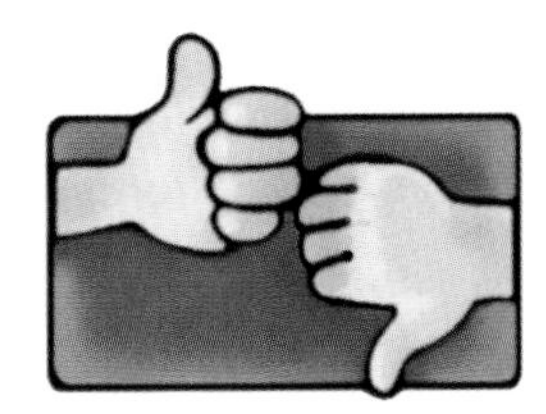

God can save us from bad things. And he can save us from sin. What would you like God to save you from?

Do a Good-Choice Activity

Taste some unleavened bread, sometimes called matzo, or a saltless cracker. Flat bread without yeast has been on the Passover tables of Jewish people ever since the first Passover. It reminds them—and us—to trust God to save us.

We can trust and obey God, who wants to save us from bad things.

Pray Together

Dear God, thank you for saving us from many bad things. Thank you most of all for sending Jesus to save us from sin. In Jesus' name. Amen.

A Dry Path

Exodus 13:17–14:31

CHOICE: Do God's people trust Moses to lead them across the sea? Or do they think it is impossible for God to help Moses?

Moses and God's people left Egypt shouting and cheering. They took their goats and donkeys. They took their cows and sheep. Not one of God's people was left behind in Egypt. All of them were going to the land of Abraham. Babies and children were going. Young people and old people were going. They were no longer slaves of the wicked pharaoh! It

must have seemed as if they were going on a huge picnic.

Back in Egypt, Pharaoh was afraid. Then he was sad. Then he was angry—really angry. He started to blame Moses for tricking him into letting the people go. He called over 600 soldiers together and went with them to find God's people. They went out in their fastest chariots and took their sharpest spears. They were going to stop Moses and bring God's people back to Egypt.

Far ahead, God was leading his people. He led them with a tall cloud during the day. At night he led them with a tall cloud of fire. At last they came to the Red Sea. There was a lot of water in front of God's people.

Some of the people turned around and saw dust in the distance. Then they saw horses. Then they saw chariots with Pharaoh and his soldiers. They were coming with spears to take God's people back to Egypt!

back. If they didn't have Moses as their leader, who could talk to God for them? Who could lead them to the land God promised them?

God's people thought that they needed another god. They remembered that the people of Egypt had lots of gods. The people of Egypt made statues, or idols, of their gods. Some were stone or clay idols. Some were gold idols. But God's people forgot that those gods were not real. Those gods had no power.

God's people brought together all of their gold

earrings. They gave their gold to Moses' brother, Aaron. They begged him to make a statue of a god so they could see their god and pray to it.

Now Aaron had a big choice to make. He could tell the people to take their gold home because Moses was coming back. He could believe that God was still with them and would take them to the land of Abraham. Or he could melt the gold to make a god the people could see. Maybe Moses really was gone forever. Maybe there would be no one to talk to God for them.

What did Aaron do? He made a huge gold calf. He let the people call it the god that had brought them from Egypt. They gave gifts to the gold calf. Then they sang and danced and ate by the calf. They worshiped it because they thought Moses wouldn't come back and talk to God for them again.

While they were worshiping the calf, Moses came back. He was so angry that he threw down the two flat stones with God's rules. He said to Aaron, "What have you done?"

"Don't be angry," said Aaron.

But Moses let Aaron know how angry God was. God was very angry about what Aaron and the people had done.

Moses went back to God. He asked God to not leave his people. When Moses came down the mountain again, he had two new flat stones. These stones had God's rules carved on them just like the first ones did.

God was pleased with Moses. So God did what Moses asked. God did not break his promise to take his people to the land of Abraham. After many years they came to the land God had promised them.

Remember Together

Why did God's people think they needed another god?

Did Aaron make a good choice or a bad choice?

What did the people do with the gold calf?

God was angry, but what did he do because he was pleased with Moses?

Think about YOUR Choices

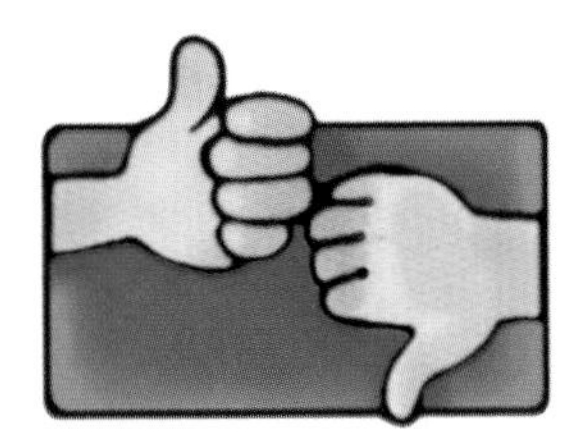

Name people or things you have to wait for (the dentist, the checkout clerk at the grocery store, Mom or Dad to come home, God to answer prayers). While you wait, how about singing Sunday school choruses or saying Bible verses?

Do a Good-Choice Activity

Play Simon Says sometime when you have to wait. If God wouldn't want you to do something, be sure not to say "Simon says." Examples: tell a lie; take something; hit someone; Simon says to smile; Simon says to sing; Simon says to hug someone.

Waiting isn't easy, but the wait doesn't seem as long when we're obeying God.

Pray Together

Dear God, help me to never stop obeying you. In Jesus' name. Amen.

Blow Your Horn

Deuteronomy 34; Joshua 6

CHOICE: Does Joshua follow God's directions at Jericho? Or does he make his own plans?

God's people walked in the desert for forty years. That's a long time! Many children grew up in the desert, and they had children of their own. Then many of the grownup people became grandparents. When they grew old, they died.

Finally Moses and God's people came to the land of Abraham. All they had to do was cross the Jordan River, and they would be in their new home.

By now Moses was very old. God let him climb a mountain, where he could look across the river. There Moses could see the new land. But then Moses died.

Moses had been a good leader, and now God had another good leader for his people. Joshua was the new leader.

Joshua led the people across the Jordan River. Then they came to the big city of Jericho. The city had a thick wall all around it. And the people inside didn't want God's people to live in the land.

Joshua knew this was the land that God had promised to his people. So Joshua listened when God

told him a secret plan. "You must lead my people around the city walls once every day for six days. On the seventh day, march around Jericho seven times. Those who have horns must blow their horns as they march. Then have all the people shout as loudly as they can. When they do that, the walls of Jericho will fall down."

Now Joshua had a big choice to make. He could obey God and line the people up to march. Some of them might think that wouldn't do any good. The people inside the walls would probably laugh at them. But it was what God said would work. Or Joshua could take the people back across the river, never letting them enjoy the land God wanted them to have. After all, the walls of Jericho did look very, very thick.

This is what Joshua did. He lined up the people. Around the city walls they marched once a day. They did this on day 1, day 2, day 3, day 4, day 5, and day 6. Those who had horns blew them.

On day 7, all the people lined up to march again. This time they went around the city seven times. Those who had horns blew them. On the seventh time around, they blew their horns hard. Then Joshua told everyone, "Now is the time! Shout!" So the people shouted as loudly as they could. When they did, the walls around Jericho fell down!

God's people could now live in the land God had promised them. God was glad that Joshua had followed his directions. God's people were glad too. Now they had their own land, and God was with them.

Remember Together

Who was the new leader after Moses died?
What did God tell Joshua to do?
Did Joshua make a good choice or a bad choice?
What happened to the walls of Jericho?

Do a Good-Choice Activity

Get some empty paper-towel tubes for horns and act out the march on Jericho. Be sure to follow all of the directions!

Think about YOUR Choices

Did your family ever pray and discover that God had an unusual solution to a problem? Was it easy to follow his directions?

When we pray, we can trust God to give us good directions.

Pray Together

Dear God, your plans are always the best ones! Thank you for all the good ideas you give people. Help us choose to follow your ways. In Jesus' name. Amen.

Traveling Together

Ruth 1–4

CHOICE: Is Ruth loving and kind to Naomi? Or does Ruth want to forget about Naomi?

Ruth was a young woman who lived near the land that God gave his people. Ruth was happy when some of God's people moved to her land. A family of four people moved to her land when their crops wouldn't grow. Ruth was happy because a young man from that family became her husband.

But many sad things happened too. The father of the family of four died. Then Ruth's husband died.

Her husband's brother also died. Then the only one left from the family of four was the mother. Her name was Naomi.

Naomi was far from her home. She heard that crops were growing in her land again. So she decided to return to her home in Bethlehem. The two young women who had been married to her sons wanted to go with her. One of these young women was Ruth. The other one was Orpah.

Naomi thought it was best for the two young women to stay in their own land. Orpah decided that

Naomi was right. So she kissed Naomi and said good-bye to her.

Now Ruth had a big choice to make. She could travel to the land of God's people with Naomi. She could live with Naomi and love God just as Naomi did. Or she could leave Naomi and go back home. She could go back to her own land and forget about God.

This is what Ruth said to Naomi. "Where you go, I will go. Your people will be my people. Your God will be my God." Naomi was very happy that she didn't have to go back home all by herself.

When they got to Bethlehem, they were tired and hungry. A kind farmer named Boaz left some grain in his field. People who needed food could gather the grain. Ruth took some of the grain and made bread so she and Naomi could eat.

Boaz noticed how kind Ruth was to Naomi. He could tell that Ruth loved her like her own mother. Boaz made sure that Ruth and Naomi had enough to eat.

Day after day Boaz saw Ruth being kind and loving to Naomi. Boaz knew this was the kind of wife he wanted. So he asked Ruth to marry him. How happy Naomi was! Now she knew Ruth would stay in the land of God's people. And she would be happy here too.

Before many years went by, a baby boy was born to Ruth and Boaz. Baby Obed was Naomi's first grandchild!

Naomi was a very happy grandmother. Boaz was a very happy father. Ruth was a very happy mother. Obed was a very happy baby.

God was very happy too. He was pleased that Ruth was so loving and kind to the family he gave her.

Remember Together

How did Ruth show that she loved Naomi?
Did Ruth make a good choice or a bad choice?
Who were the people in Ruth's new family?

Think about YOUR Choices

Name one kind or loving thing you can do for each member of your family. How can your family share what you have with hungry people? They live nearer to you than you think!

Do a Good-Choice Activity

Families get separated by years and miles and sometimes by arguments. But God wants families to show love for each other. Choose to call or write someone you love today.

God is pleased when families do kind things for each other.

Pray Together

Dear God, thank you for our family. Help us to love each other the way you love us. In Jesus' name. Amen.

"Please Send Me a Son"

1 Samuel 1:1–2:21

CHOICE: Does Hannah believe that God will answer her prayers for help? Or does she think it won't matter if she prays?

Hannah was so sad. She had a nice home that she kept neat and tidy. And she had a good, strong husband. But Hannah did not have a baby. So Hannah was sad.

Every year Hannah and her husband went to a special place to pray. They went to a big tent called a tabernacle. All of God's people went there to worship

God. The time had come for them to go to this special place again.

Now Hannah had a big choice to make. She could go and pray to God. She could tell God just how she felt. And she could believe that God would hear her and answer her prayers. Or she could stay home and just feel sad. She had prayed for a baby for so long, and still there was no baby. Maybe God did not hear her prayers.

What did Hannah do? She went with her husband to the special worship place. She went to the special

tent to pray alone. She told God how sad she was. She told him that she felt so alone when other women talked about their babies. She thanked God for her husband and for her home. But she asked God to please, please, please send her a baby.

Then Hannah made a promise to God. She promised that if she had a baby, she would have him help God all of his life. As soon as her son was old enough, he would help right here at the Tabernacle.

Eli worked at the Tabernacle. He sat near the place where Hannah was praying and crying. He told her that her prayers would be answered.

Hannah went back home feeling happy. She did not have a baby yet. But she was happy that she had prayed. She was glad she told God just how she felt.

Before another year went by, Hannah's baby was born! God had heard her prayers! Hannah loved her baby and named him Samuel. She counted his fingers and toes. She rocked him to sleep. She gave him baths and fed him.

One day Samuel was old enough to help at the Tabernacle. So Hannah and her husband took him to Eli. Samuel worked with Eli to help God. Samuel was a good helper.

Every year Hannah made a new coat for Samuel. She praised God for giving her a wonderful son.

Hannah was glad that she had prayed for a son. God was glad that Hannah had believed he would answer her prayers. He took good care of little Samuel. The boy grew up and helped God all of his life, just as Hannah had promised he would.

Remember Together

Why was Hannah sad?
Where did she go to pray?
Did Hannah make a good choice or a bad choice?
How did God answer Hannah's prayer?
How did Samuel help God?

Think about YOUR Choices

What things do you pray for? Does God always answer your prayers by giving you what you want? Sometimes God may say, "Wait!" Sometimes he may say, "No!" Remember that those are answers too.

Do a Good-Choice Activity

Choose a neighbor or a family you know, and pray for them every night this week. Ask God to give them what they need. Trust God to give the right answer at the right time!

Praying is always the right thing to do!

Pray Together

Dear God, thanks for letting us tell you exactly what we want and just how we feel. Thanks for listening and caring. Thanks for knowing exactly how and when to answer our prayers. In Jesus' name. Amen.

The Big, Big Soldier

1 Samuel 17

CHOICE: Is David brave? Or is he afraid of Goliath?

"David! David!"

Far off in the sheep meadow, David sat playing his harp and singing about God's world. At first he didn't hear the voice. He was remembering the time he had chased a lion away from the sheep. The lion had run away when he threw stones at it, using his little sling.

Then the voice was louder. "David, come home!"

David grabbed his sling and ran home. His father said, "I want you to go to your older brothers." The brothers were fighting in a big army. David's father wanted to know how they were. And he wanted them to have bread and cheese and other food.

So David set off to see his brothers. He took along the food his father gave him and his sling.

David found his brothers and the other men in the army. Right away, he knew that they needed help to be brave. Most of the time they were brave men, but now they were afraid. One man in the other army was so big that no one would fight him. His name was Goliath, and he was huge—he was a giant! Everything about

Goliath was very big. He had huge hands and huge arms. And he was very tall!

Now David had a big choice to make. He could be brave and fight Goliath, knowing that God would be with him. Or he could go back home. After all, Goliath was really, really big.

This is what David did. He told the soldiers he would

fight Goliath. He said to the king, "God kept me safe from a lion. He can keep me safe from this giant, too."

King Saul said, "You're just a boy." But when the king heard how brave David was, he said, "Go ahead. And God be with you."

David didn't want to wear the metal armor that the king offered him. And he didn't know how to use a sword. He told the king that he would wear his own clothes and carry only his little sling.

David found five smooth stones by a stream of water. Then he went to meet Goliath.

When Goliath saw this shepherd boy, he laughed so hard that he didn't see David put a stone in his sling. He didn't see David spin it around real fast. He didn't know what was happening until the stone hit him—*smack*—in the head and knocked him over.

When David's brothers and all the other soldiers saw Goliath fall, they felt brave again. If David could fight a giant, they could face anyone. That day they won the battle. Hooray for David!

God was pleased that David was brave. And David was glad that he had trusted God to help him.

Remember Together

Why were the soldiers afraid?
Why did David think he could fight Goliath?
Did David make a good choice or a bad choice?
What happened to the big, big man?

Think about YOUR Choices

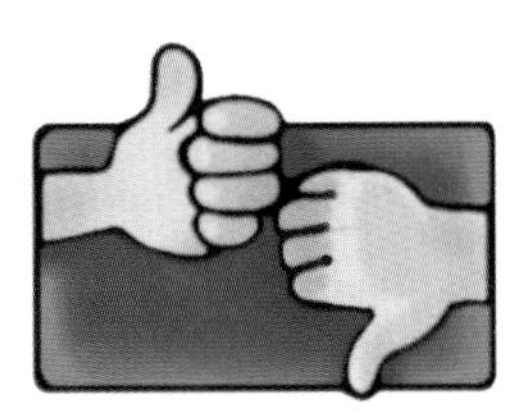

How does your family handle bullies at school? in the neighborhood? on the expressway? God's plan for David was to use his sling, but his plan for us might be very different. It might simply be to ignore a bully, to report a fight to an adult, or to pray for an unkind person.

Do a Good-Choice Activity

Find library books about ways animals can protect themselves (deer, porcupines, skunks, etc.). God made animals so they can be safe. God takes care of us, too!

We can choose to be brave and believe that God will keep us safe.

Pray Together

Dear God, help us choose to be brave and trust you. We know you'll show us how to stay safe. In Jesus' name. Amen.

Friends Forever

1 Samuel 18:1-4; 20

CHOICE: Is Jonathan a true friend? Or won't he help David?

David and Jonathan were not alike. David took care of sheep. Jonathan was the son of the king. David had a sling to hunt with. Jonathan had a bow and arrow. David was poor. Jonathan was rich. But somehow they became best friends.

One day Jonathan's father, King Saul, became very angry at David, so David had to hide from King Saul. David and Jonathan didn't understand. David hadn't done anything wrong. Jonathan didn't want David to get in trouble. He didn't want his father to hurt David.

Now Jonathan had a big choice to make. He could try to find out why his father was so angry. And he

could find a way to help David so his friend would be safe. Or Jonathan could tell his father where David was. And he could forget about being David's friend.

This is what Jonathan did. He thought of a plan to save his friend. He told David, "Hide behind the big pile of stones while I talk to my father. Then I'll come out and shoot three arrows. I'll send a boy to pick them up. If I tell him to bring the arrows to me, that means you'll be safe. My father won't hurt you. But if I tell the boy to keep going to find the arrows, that means you're not safe. You'll have to go away."

Jonathan talked to his father. He could see that it was not safe for David to come back. So he shot three arrows and said, “Hurry. Go quickly.” The boy with Jonathan picked up the arrows and went back to town.

David came out from where he was hiding long enough to say good-bye to Jonathan. The young men were sad. But they promised to be friends forever and ever, no matter what. And they were!

God was happy that Jonathan was David’s good friend. And God took care of David while the angry king looked for him.

Remember Together

Who was David's friend?
How did Saul feel about David?
What was Jonathan's plan to save David?
Did Jonathan make a good choice or a bad choice?

Think about YOUR Choices

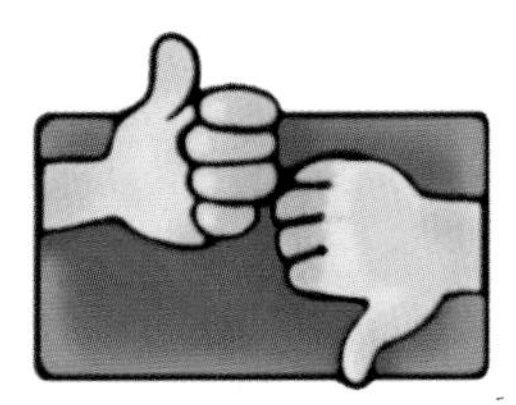

Name some of your friends. What do you like to do together? How are you alike? not alike? What are some ways you and your friends help each other?

Do a Good-Choice Activity

Draw a stick figure on paper and label the parts of a person who chooses to be a friend: helping hand, loving heart, lips that speak kind words, etc.

God gives us friends and wants us to be kind to them.

Pray Together

Dear God, please take good care of all our friends. Show us how to be kind and helpful to them. In Jesus' name. Amen.

Even Kings Do Wrong Things

2 Samuel 11–12:10; Psalm 51

CHOICE: Is King David sorry about what he has done wrong? Or will he not admit that he did anything wrong?

David had to hide from King Saul for a long time. But after Saul died, David became the next king!

David tried to be a good king and do what was right. He talked often to God, and he did what he could to help his people. He was a kind king.

But there were times when King David did things that were wrong. David thought that the wife of one of his soldiers was very beautiful. He wanted her so much that he had her husband killed. Then he married her.

God was very unhappy with David, but God still loved him. So God asked a man named Nathan to talk to David about what he had done.

Nathan went to see the king. Nathan told a story to help David see what he had done wrong. Nathan said, "A poor man had just one little lamb. A rich man had a lot of big sheep and little lambs. But the rich man took the one little lamb from the poor man."

David was angry when he heard that story. He wanted to find that rich man. "That man must pay back the poor man," he said.

Nathan said, "That man is you, David. You had so much, but you took another man's wife to be your own."

Now David had a big choice to make. He could admit that he had done something very wrong. And he could be sorry about it. Or he could pretend that he never did anything wrong.

This is what David did. He stopped in the middle of his anger. How bad David felt about the wrong thing he had done. David knew that he had sinned against God. So David prayed, letting God know how very sorry he was. He asked God to forgive him. And God did!

God was sad that David had sinned. But God was glad that David listened to Nathan. Now that David was sorry about what he had done wrong, he could be a better king.

Remember Together

How did David make God unhappy?
What did God ask Nathan to do?
How did Nathan's story help David?
Did David make a good choice or a bad choice?

Think about YOUR Choices

Sometimes you might think you can hide the things you do wrong. Is there anything you can keep from God? The sooner you talk to God about the wrong things you've done, the sooner he can forgive you!

Do a Good-Choice Activity

Cover a paper with colors that show how you feel (and how God feels) when you've done a wrong thing. Cover another paper with colors that show how you feel (and how God feels) after you've told God you're sorry.

God forgives us when we're sorry for the wrong things we've done.

Pray Together

Dear God, all of us—from kids to kings—sometimes choose to do things that are wrong. Right now, I need to have you forgive me for ________. Thank you! In Jesus' name. Amen.

The Best Gift

1 Kings 3

CHOICE: Does Solomon choose the gift of wisdom? Or does he ask for a gift that isn't as important?

David had a son named Solomon. One day it was Solomon's turn to be the king.

Solomon loved God and worshiped him. One night God talked to Solomon in a dream. God said, "Ask me for whatever you want, and I will give it to you."

Solomon might have thought that it would be nice to be rich. Then he could have anything he wanted. Having a lot of money would be very nice.

Then Solomon probably thought about how good it would be to be really wise. He wouldn't just want to be smart and know a lot of things. If Solomon was wise, he would want to be able to make good choices.

Remember Together

What did God tell Solomon that he could have?

What did Solomon ask God to give him?

Did Solomon make a good choice or a bad choice?

What did God do for Solomon?

Think about YOUR Choices

Think about some gifts God has already given you: Can you run fast? Do you like to sing or draw? Are you good at learning new things? How can you use these gifts to help other people?

Do a Good-Choice Activity

Whenever you need to make a decision this week, ask God to help you be wise. At the end of the week, you and your family can make a list of wise choices God helped you make.

God is wise, and he wants to help us be wise too.

Pray Together

Dear God, help us choose to be wise and caring like Solomon. In Jesus' name. Amen.

A Little Wheat

1 Kings 17:7-16

CHOICE: Does a woman share her food with Elijah? Or does she keep it all for herself?

The sun was hot on Elijah's head. He was hungry and thirsty. There had been no rain in the land for a long time. No rain to fill the streams with water to drink. No rain to grow wheat for flour. No rain to help the olive trees grow olives for oil.

God told Elijah to go to a town far away. God said that a woman there could give him food.

So Elijah walked to the town. When he got there, he saw a woman picking up sticks. He asked, "Would you bring me some water and bread?

But the woman said, "I have just enough flour and oil to make bread for myself and my son one more time."

Elijah said, "Don't be afraid to bake some bread for me, too. God told me that your flour and oil will last until it rains again."

Now the woman had a big choice to make. She could bake the bread for Elijah and trust God to help her and her son have enough to eat. Or she could send Elijah away and bake the last bread for herself and her son.

This is what the woman did. She baked some bread and took it to Elijah. He ate it all and told her to make

more. Just as Elijah had promised, there was plenty of flour and oil to bake bread for herself and her son.

Every day the woman baked bread for the three of them. And every day there was more flour and oil in the jars. God made sure that there was enough until the rain came. Then wheat and olives could grow again, and people everywhere could make all the food they needed.

God was glad that the woman shared her food and trusted him to take care of her family and Elijah.

Remember Together

Why was Elijah hungry?

What did God tell Elijah to do?

What did Elijah tell the woman when she was afraid to share?

Did the woman make a good choice or a bad choice?

How did God take care of Elijah, the woman, and her son?

Think about YOUR Choices

Did you ever almost run out of anything (flour, gasoline, money, etc.), and God helped you have enough? What do you think God might want you to share with someone? Food? Clothes? Books? Toys?

Do a Good-Choice Activity

Work with your church or a local welfare agency to discover if something might be needed that you can share. Or thank a person who shared something with you.

It pleases God when we share what we have with others.

Pray Together

Dear God, help us choose to share the things you give us. Thank you for always making sure that we have enough. In Jesus' name. Amen.

Seven Baths in One Day

2 Kings 5

> **CHOICE:** Does a young girl help Naaman? Or does she keep quiet about who can help him get well?

Naaman was an important man in the army. He was a good man and very brave.

But Naaman had a terrible sickness, and no one could make him well. All over his skin were sores that hurt and looked bad. Naaman wished that someone could help him.

Now there was a young girl who lived at Naaman's house. This girl helped Naaman's wife. She had come from the land where God's people lived. She loved God and knew other people who loved him too. She knew about a man named Elisha. He was one of God's helpers.

Naaman and his wife were good to the young girl.

So she felt sad when she learned about Naaman's sickness. She thought about God's helper named Elisha. She knew that Elisha would know what to do.

Naaman's wife called for her young helper. So the girl went to see what she wanted.

Now the young girl had a big choice to make. She could tell Naaman's wife about Elisha. She could say that he loved God and helped to make people well. Or she could keep quiet. After all, she was just a young girl. And she was from another land. No one would think that she could help an important man like Naaman.

This is what the young girl did. She told Naaman's wife, "I know a man who loves God. His name is Elisha. Your husband should go to see him. I know Elisha could help make your husband well again."

When Naaman heard that there might be someone who could help him, he was happy! He and his helpers took his fastest horses and chariot. They drove to Elisha's house.

Elisha said that Naaman should take seven baths in the Jordan River. Then his skin would be well.

Naaman was upset. He had washed his skin at home, and it didn't make him well. But his helpers said, "If Elisha had asked you to do a great thing, you would have done it gladly. What harm could come from washing seven times? And it might make you well."

So Naaman went down to the Jordan River. He went into the water and rinsed off his skin one time. There was no difference. He did it a second time. There was no difference. He did it a third time and a

fourth and a fifth and a sixth time. There was no change in his skin at all. He stepped into the water for the seventh time and came out. He looked at his arms. There were no sores. There were none on his legs or his hands or his head. Naaman was well!

God was pleased that the young girl told Naaman's wife about Elisha. Naaman was happy about it too. He thanked Elisha. And he learned to love God because of what the young girl did.

Remember Together

What did the young girl know that could help Naaman?

Did the girl make a good choice or a bad choice?

What did Elisha tell Naaman to do?

What good things happened because of what the girl did?

Think about YOUR Choices

Did you know that you're not too young to help people know about God? You can tell people how much you love God's Son, Jesus! You can show them your Bible storybooks and sing your Sunday school songs and say your favorite Bible verses. You can pray for them too. Name someone you might be able to help this week.

Do a Good-Choice Activity

Choose one of the above ideas and do it for someone this week.

God is pleased when children choose to help people know about him.

Pray Together

Dear God, show me how to help someone know you better. In Jesus' name. Amen.

"Now, Listen!"

2 Kings 22–23

CHOICE: Does Josiah read God's Word to his people? Or does he think that God's laws aren't important?

Josiah was eight years old, and he had a special job to do. He was the king! He wanted to be a good king. He wanted to do what was right. He didn't just want to do what seemed right to him. He wanted to do what God said was right. And that's what he did as he grew up.

When Josiah became a young man, he saw that the Temple needed fixing. And the things that didn't belong there needed to be carried away. So many workers came to fix the Temple and clean it up.

As the Temple was being fixed, workers found some scrolls. The scrolls belonged at the Temple. But for years and years, no one had known about them. The scrolls, which were like rolled-up pieces of paper, had laws written on them. These were the good laws of God that he had given to Moses so long ago.

One of the king's helpers took the scrolls to King Josiah. The man read some of God's laws to the king. Josiah was upset. He knew that the people had not obeyed God's laws for years and years.

Now Josiah had a big choice to make. He could read all of God's laws and learn how to obey them. And he could call the people together and read the laws to them. Then they would also know how to obey God again. Or he could tell his helper to take the scrolls away. He could say that he didn't think God's laws were important.

What did Josiah do? He called the people together. He stood by a tall pillar at the Temple and began to read. The people listened. They learned about God's laws and his love and his promises. The king and his people made a promise: They promised to love God and obey his laws.

It was right that the people wanted to love and obey God again. It was good that Josiah found God's laws and shared them with everyone.

Remember Together

What had been lost at the Temple?

Why was King Josiah upset?

Did Josiah make a good choice or a bad choice?

What did the people promise to do when they heard God's laws?

Think about YOUR Choices

How often do you listen to Bible stories or read Bible storybooks? What should you want to do when you hear God's Word?

Do a Good-Choice Activity

Make a Bible scroll by taping several pieces of paper together. On the paper, write a favorite Bible verse or two. Tape one end to a paper-towel tube and roll the scroll around it. You may also write a favorite Bible story in your own words and draw a picture for your story. Read the story to your family.

Reading God's Word helps us know how to love and obey him.

Pray Together

Dear God, thank you for the Bible. Thank you that we can choose to read and hear your Word. We love you! In Jesus' name. Amen.

Who's Afraid of Lions?

Daniel 6

CHOICE: Does Daniel keep praying to God? Or does he stop praying?

"Roar!" The sound of lions filled the city streets. They were hungry lions, ready for dinner.

Daniel and his friends heard the lions roar too. They knew that there was a cave full of lions. Sometimes people were thrown into the cave with the lions. That's what happened to people who did not obey the king.

Daniel was a good friend of the king. He was one of the king's most important helpers. In fact, the king keep on praying to God just as he had always done. Then he would probably have to spend the night with the lions. Daniel didn't have to wonder what hungry lions could do to him. Or Daniel could just obey the king's law. Then he would have to stop praying to God and worship the king. Maybe he could pretend to pray to him but not really mean it in his heart.

What did Daniel do? He kept right on praying to God every day. He didn't just pray one time each day. He didn't just pray two times each day. He prayed three times every day! And he didn't try to hide when

he prayed. In fact, he prayed right by an open window where everyone could see him!

Of course, the king's other helpers did see Daniel. And, of course, they went to tell the king what they saw. The king was very sad. He didn't really want to let the lions hurt Daniel. He tried to think of a way to save his friend. But the law he had signed couldn't be changed. So the other helpers grabbed Daniel. At sunset they put him in the cave with the lions.

The king couldn't sleep at all that night. He

wondered how Daniel was doing. As soon as it was light, the king ran as fast as he could to the cave. He called, "Daniel, was God able to save you from the lions?"

The king looked inside the cave. Then he rubbed his eyes and looked again. There was Daniel with the hungry lions, and he had not been hurt by any of them!

"God sent an angel," said Daniel. "He closed the lions' mouths so they couldn't hurt me. God knew that I had done nothing wrong."

How happy the king was that Daniel was all right. God was happy too. Daniel had obeyed God's laws. That was the right thing to do, and that's what Daniel wanted to do.

Remember Together

Why did the king make a new law?

Why was the new law a bad law?

Did Daniel make a good choice or a bad choice?

What kind of animal was in the cave?

How did God take care of Daniel?

Think about YOUR Choices

What are some times when God wants you to talk to him? Is it ever hard to pray to God? Do you ever forget to pray? You can ask God to help you remember!

Do a Good-Choice Activity

Daniel prayed, and God kept him safe from hungry lions. Act out ways that God can keep you safe when you pray (pretend to ride a bike, run from a mean dog, etc.).

When we pray, we're obeying one of God's laws—and that's good!

Pray Together

Dear God, help us always choose to obey your laws and love you most of all. In Jesus' name. Amen.

Traveling by Fish

Jonah 1–2

CHOICE: Does Jonah want to be God's helper? Or does he try to run away?

God said to Jonah, "I have a job for you. I want you to help the people in the city of Nineveh. They are doing many wrong things. I want them to love and obey me. I want them to love each other, too."

Now Jonah had a big choice to make. He could go to Nineveh and do what God said. The people of Nineveh might not want to see him. But he would be doing what God wanted him to do. Or Jonah could say no to God. He could decide that he didn't want to do this job.

What did Jonah do? He decided to run away! He ran down to the sea and got on a ship. It was not going anywhere near the city of Nineveh. It was going the other direction. Maybe Jonah thought that God wouldn't find him if he was out on the sea. But God knew right where Jonah was.

God sent a big storm with a strong wind. Big waves pounded against the ship. The other men had never seen a storm this bad. Jonah knew that God had sent the storm. And Jonah knew what he had to do.

Jonah told the other men, "I've been running away

from God. So he sent the storm. If you throw me into the sea, the storm will stop." The men didn't want to do it. But they knew they had to, so they did. Right away the storm stopped, and all the men on the ship were safe.

But Jonah didn't know what was going to happen to him. He could see only water and all kinds of strange fish—little tiny purple fish, medium-sized yellow fish, and one huge fish. It was so big that it swallowed other fish whole. It was so big that it swallowed Jonah whole!

Now Jonah was inside the fish, and he began to pray. He knew that God had sent the big fish to save him. So he thanked God and promised to obey him.

What happened next? The fish swam up to the shore. It opened its mouth, and out poured all kinds of little fish. Out came Jonah, too, right onto the sandy beach. Jonah was so happy!

Once again, God asked Jonah to go to Nineveh. This time Jonah knew right away what choice he would make. He would obey God and go to Nineveh.

The people at Nineveh listened to Jonah. They were

sorry about the wrong things they were doing. They decided to change the way they were living. They would love each other. And they would love God most of all.

God was happy that Jonah finally obeyed him and became his helper. God was glad that the people of Nineveh wanted to love and obey him too.

Remember Together

Where did God want Jonah to go?

Did Jonah make a good choice or a bad choice?

After Jonah got out of the fish, what kind of choice did he make?

What did the people of Nineveh do when they heard Jonah?

Think about YOUR Choices

Maybe you don't want to obey God sometimes. You might not want to pray. Perhaps you don't feel like being kind. Or maybe you don't want to obey your parents. What sad things happen then?

Do a Good-Choice Activity

At bedtime, hide under the covers. That's how dark it was inside the fish. Shake the bed and pretend the fish swims. Now throw back the covers. How good to be in the light again! Obeying God is like being in the light, where we're safe and happy.

Obeying God is better than running away from doing what's right.

Pray Together

Dear God, help us not to run away from doing what's right. In Jesus' name. Amen.

God's Surprising Plan

Luke 1:26-50

CHOICE: Does Mary agree to do what God wants? Or doesn't she want to be part of his plan?

Mary lived in the little town of Nazareth. Like other girls, she got water at the well for her mother. She learned to cook and sew, too. Mary was kind to the animals and always gave bread crumbs to the birds.

Mary grew up and was going to get married! Her husband would be Joseph. He had a carpenter shop and made all kinds of nice furniture. What a pretty house Mary would have! Mary began to think about

her wedding and the big party they would have to celebrate.

As Mary was sweeping the floor one morning, a stranger appeared in the room. His clothes were so white, they seemed to shine. Mary had never seen anyone like him before. She was afraid.

The stranger was really an angel. His name was Gabriel, and God had sent him.

The angel said, “Don’t be afraid, Mary. I have good news for you.”

Perhaps Mary thought the good news was about Joseph or the wedding.

The angel said, "God is ready to send the Savior into the world. He will tell everyone about God's love. God wants you to be the mother of this very special baby. He wants you to name the baby Jesus."

Mary was puzzled. She said, "I can't have a baby. I'm not married to Joseph yet."

The angel said, "This baby will be God's own Son. He will save people from their sins."

Now Mary had a big choice to make. She could agree to do what God wanted. Then she would have to believe that God would take care of her, even if Joseph didn't understand. Or she could tell the angel that she didn't want to be part of God's plan. He would have to find another mother for this baby.

What *did* Mary do? She said to the angel, "I am glad to do what God asks."

After the angel left, Mary went to visit her cousin Elizabeth. Right away, Elizabeth knew that something was very different. She knew that Mary was going to have a very special baby.

Mary sang a song. She sang, "My heart is full of praise for God. He is doing a wonderful thing. He is sending a baby into the world. And he has chosen me to be the mother of this baby."

God was pleased that Mary wanted to be part of his plan. She would do what he wanted her to do. She would be the mother of his Son, baby Jesus.

Remember Together

Who was Mary going to marry?

What did the angel say God wanted Mary to do?

Did Mary make a good choice or a bad choice?

What did Mary do after the angel left?

How did Mary feel about God's plan for her?

Think about YOUR Choices

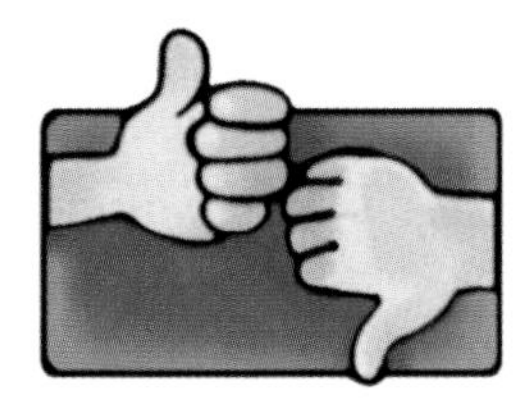

What does God want *you* to do? God wants you to obey your parents and teachers. He wants you to learn new things. And he wants you to be kind. Will you do what God wants you to do?

Do a Good-Choice Activity

Draw a picture of something you did today that God wanted you to do. As you draw, think about what God might want you to do when you grow up.

God is glad when we follow his plans for us.

Pray Together

Dear God, we want to obey you and talk to you every day. We want you to show us your plans for us. In Jesus' name. Amen.

Taking Care of Mary and Jesus

Matthew 1:18-25

CHOICE: Does Joseph take care of Mary and Jesus? Or doesn't he do what God wants?

Joseph had a carpenter shop in Nazareth. He had a saw and hammers. Every day he made things from wood for other people. Sometimes he made tables and benches. Sometimes he fixed farmers' tools. Joseph was very busy and very happy.

He was especially happy now because he was going to be married. He knew that Mary was kind and helpful. How nice it would be to have her share his home. Joseph thought of the table he would make for his own house and his own wife.

One day Mary had surprising news for Joseph! Mary told him that an angel had come to visit her. Then she told him that she was going to have a baby. Joseph didn't know what to think. He didn't know what to say.

As he walked home, perhaps Joseph thought about all the plans he had made. He had planned for Mary to be his wife. And he had planned that they would have children. But now . . .

That night, Joseph was all alone in his little house. He didn't think that he and Mary could get married now. When he went to bed, he must have felt that all his hopes were gone.

But Joseph had a dream that night. An angel talked to Joseph in his dream. The angel had an important message from God. The angel said, "Don't be afraid to let Mary be your wife. Don't be afraid to take care of her and the baby. The child that Mary will have is the Son of God. Name him Jesus. He will save people from their sins."

Joseph woke up with a start just as the sun was coming up.

Now Joseph had a big choice to make. He could take Mary to be his wife. And he could raise the baby Jesus, knowing he was God's Son. Or he could quietly send Mary away to another village. He could let her raise the baby herself. After all, he was just a carpenter. Taking care of this special baby would be a job that was much too important.

What did Joseph do? He threw on his clothes and

probably ran all the way to Mary's house. He told her about the dream and the angel. He promised to take care of Mary and the baby.

So Mary and Joseph went on with their plans to be married. Together they would live in the little house with the carpenter shop. Together they would raise the baby Jesus.

God was happy that Joseph was going to take care of Mary and the baby. God knew that his Son, Jesus, would be safe with Joseph.

Remember Together

What kind of work did Joseph do?

Was Joseph happy to be getting married?

What was the surprising news that Mary had for him?

What did the angel say in Joseph's dream?

Did Joseph make a good choice or a bad choice?

Think about YOUR Choices

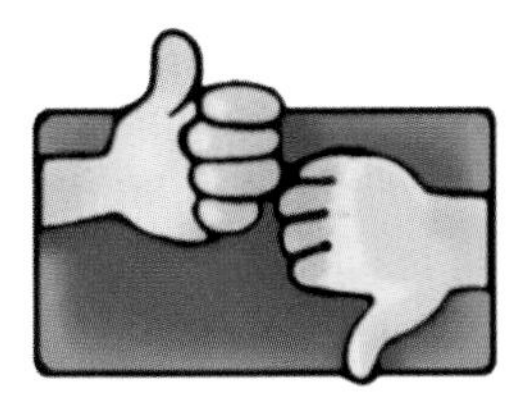

What are some of the jobs God gives to the different people in your family? Do your jobs seem too hard sometimes? Remember that if God wants you to do something, he will help you do it!

Do a Good-Choice Activity

Choose to call someone who has taken care of a family member in the past—a grandparent, baby-sitter, teacher—just to say thanks.

God will always help people do the jobs he gives them to do.

Pray Together

Dear God, thank you for all the people who help you take care of us. Thanks for the jobs you give *us* to do too. In Jesus' name. Amen.

"Don't Be Afraid"

Luke 2:8-20

CHOICE: Do the shepherds believe the angels? Or don't the shepherds listen to them?

The shepherds on the hills outside Bethlehem watched their sheep all day. But they saw other things too. They saw a Roman soldier ride his fast horse to Bethlehem. The shepherds knew he was coming to count all the people who had been born here. And all day long they watched the people who were coming back to their city to be counted.

Late in the day a tired couple came up the path to the town. The woman was riding a little donkey, and the man looked very worried. By evening, so many people had come that it seemed as if the walls around the town would burst. The shepherds wondered where all of the people would sleep. There weren't enough beds in Bethlehem. That must be why the tired man looked worried.

When evening came, the shepherds counted all of their sheep. Then they settled down for the night.

It was a quiet night in the field where the sheep were. The shepherds talked softly about the weather. They ate their supper. And they put branches on a fire to keep the wolves away. The sheep slept on the hillside. Some of the shepherds slept too.

Suddenly a bright light filled the sky! It may have been the youngest shepherd who saw it first and woke the others. They all stared as the light became brighter and brighter. Soon they could see an angel. The sky was so bright now that the night was no longer dark at all. What could this mean? The shepherds pulled up the hoods of their cloaks. Perhaps some even hid behind rocks.

The angel had an important message: “Don’t be afraid. I have good news for everyone. The Savior has

been born in Bethlehem. You can go see. Just look for a newborn baby wrapped up in cloth. You'll find him sleeping with the animals."

Suddenly the whole sky was full of angels! They were all praising God, saying, "Glory to God!"

Then, just as quickly as they had come, they were gone. There were no angels, there was no praising in the sky, and there was no bright light. There were just sleepy sheep and shepherds—some perhaps peeking out from behind rocks. The youngest shepherd wondered what they were going to do.

Now the shepherds had a big choice to make. They could believe the angels and do what the angels said. They could go to Bethlehem and look for a baby sleeping with the animals. Or they could act as if this night were like every other night. They could stay and watch the sheep. They could pretend the angels never came.

This is what they did. They talked to each other in excited voices. They knew that the angels had come from God. So they said, "Let's go to Bethlehem and find the baby. Let's see for ourselves what God has told us about." They probably chose one or two

shepherds to stay and watch the sheep. The rest of them ran to Bethlehem as fast as they could. The youngest shepherd ran with them.

They found a little stable that had animals in it. A man, a woman, and a newborn baby were in the stable too. It was all just as the angel had said.

The shepherds tiptoed in and looked at the baby. He was a beautiful baby, sleeping peacefully.

When it was time to go, the shepherds were too excited to go right back to their sheep. Instead, they told everyone they met about the angels and the wonderful news: Jesus the Savior of the world was born!

God was happy that the shepherds believed the angels. He was glad that the shepherds were the first ones to find his Son, baby Jesus.

Remember Together

What were the shepherds doing?
What did the angel tell them to do?
Did the shepherds make a good choice or a bad choice?
Who did they find sleeping with the animals?

Think about YOUR Choices

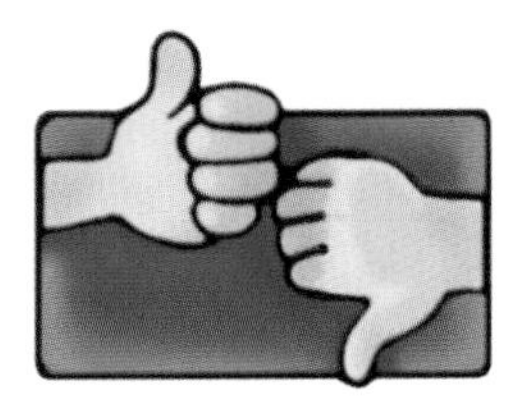

God tells us in the Bible that Jesus is with us all the time! Will you believe that? Will you tell him right now that you love him?

Do a Good-Choice Activity

Put on bathrobes and sandals. Get out some cotton balls for sheep and a flashlight for the bright angels. Have fun playing shepherds.

We can believe what the Bible says about Jesus, just as the shepherds believed the angel.

Pray Together

Dear God, thank you for sending Jesus into the world for shepherds and for us! Help us to believe that you are with us and that we can talk to you anytime. In Jesus' name. Amen.

The New Star

Matthew 2:1-11

CHOICE: Do the wise men believe that God will lead them? Or do they stay home?

Jesus was born in the little town of Bethlehem. Not many people knew about the town or the baby. But far away to the east, wise men knew something wonderful had taken place.

These men watched the stars every night. One night they saw a new star, brighter and more beautiful than any other. And they knew that a new king had come. He would be the king of all the people, even wise men who lived far away.

The star was new, and it appeared in the western sky. That's all the wise men knew. They didn't know the name of the king or where to find him.

Now the wise men had a big choice to make. They could travel in the direction of the star. Then they would need to trust God to lead them to the new king. Or they could stay in their homes and keep on studying the stars. They could write about the new star that they saw but never know who the new king was.

This is what happened. The men got ready for the long trip and packed everything they needed. They took food and clothes and gifts—great gifts for an important king. They watched for the star in the west, and they rode toward it.

It took a long time to find the king. Every day they

slept, and every night they followed the star. The star seemed to move in the sky, leading them to the king.

When the men came to Jerusalem, they thought surely a king would be born in a big city like this. So they asked, "Where is the new king? We followed his star all the way here."

King Herod did not know where the little king was. He called his wisest men, and they looked in all their scrolls. Finally they said, "He is in Bethlehem."

King Herod talked to the wise men about the star. Then he told them to look for the young child in Bethlehem.

The men went outside. Once again the star traveled in front of them, leading them to Bethlehem. There, in a little house, they found Jesus with his mother, Mary.

When they saw him, the wise men worshiped him. Then they showed him the gifts they had brought. There were shining gold and sweet perfume and special spices. The wise men told Mary all about the wonderful star and their long trip to find the little king.

God was happy that the wise men wanted to see Jesus. God was glad that they followed the star he put in the sky. Jesus would be their king!

Remember Together

What did the wise men see in the sky?
What good choice did the wise men make?
Where did the star lead them?
What did they do when they found Jesus?

Think about YOUR Choices

We may not have a star to follow, but we can always pray for God to lead us. Will you follow God wherever he wants you to go?

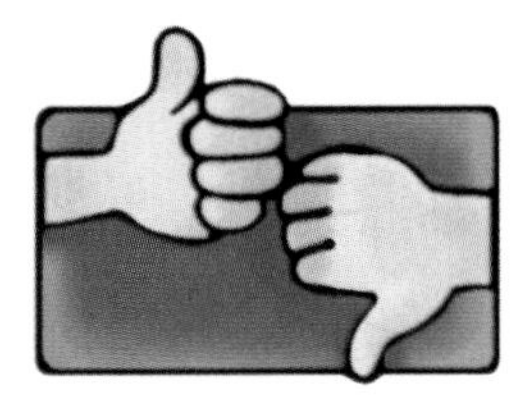

Do a Good-Choice Activity

On a clear night, look at the stars with someone from your family. There are a lot of them, aren't there? How could the wise men have seen a new one? God must have helped them find it.

We can choose to follow God wherever he leads us.

Pray Together

Dear God, thank you for sending your star to lead the wise men to your Son. Help us choose to follow you too. Most of all, we want to worship your Son, Jesus, just as the wise men did. In his name. Amen.

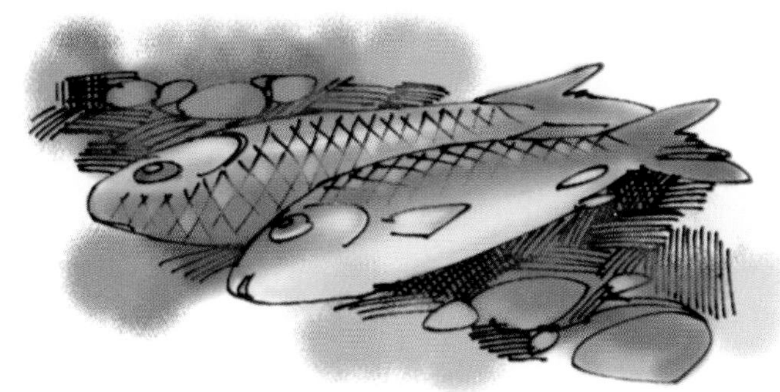

Leave the Fish

Mark 1:16-20

CHOICE: Do Peter, Andrew, James, and John follow Jesus? Or do they keep fishing?

It was very early in the morning, just as the sun was coming up. Some fishing boats were out on the Sea of Galilee. Fishermen had been fishing all night. In one boat were two brothers, Peter and Andrew. In another boat were two other brothers, James and John. The four men had been fishermen for a long time, and they often went out to fish at night. They came back to shore early every morning.

The men fished with nets. They would put a big net into the boat. Then they would row out onto the sea. They would throw the net into the water, holding on to the edges. Fish would swim into the net and be caught. When there were a lot of fish in the net, the fishermen would dump all the fish into the boat. Then they would take the fish home. They would eat some of the fish themselves. But they would trade the rest of the fish with other people to get bread and fruit.

After the brothers threw their nets into the water, they would have to wait. Sometimes they took a nap. Sometimes they watched the gulls flying overhead. Sometimes they watched the people on shore.

One day they saw a man walking alone on the beach. It was Jesus! He was now a grown-up man. He called out to Peter and Andrew, “Follow me, and I’ll let you fish for people.” Then he asked James and John to follow him.

The brothers looked at each other. They weren’t sure what “fishing for people” meant.

But something made the fishermen feel that God was calling them to follow Jesus. They all felt it, and they knew it was what God wanted them to do.

Now Peter and Andrew and James and John had a big choice to make. They could listen to God and

follow Jesus. Or they could keep rowing their boats and fishing.

What did the fishermen do? Peter and his brother, Andrew, dropped the nets they were holding. All the fish they had caught swam away into the sea. James and his brother, John, dropped their nets too. The four fishermen rowed and rowed for the shore as fast as they could. They ran across the beach to Jesus.

Peter and Andrew and James and John promised to follow Jesus and be his best friends. They would learn from him and be his disciples. They would find people instead of fish. Then they could teach the people about God's love.

God was glad that Peter and Andrew and James and John wanted to follow Jesus. He knew they would be good helpers.

Remember Together

How many brothers were in each boat?
Who did they see on the shore?
What did Jesus ask them to fish for?
Did the four fishermen make a good choice or a bad choice?

Think about YOUR Choices

Jesus wants you to be his helper too. But first you must learn from him, just as the fishermen did. How will you learn? How will you help?

Do a Good-Choice Activity

Use watercolor paints to make a picture of the boats on the water. For more fun, spread glue along the bottom of the picture and sprinkle sand on it for the beach. Or just eat some fish-shaped crackers!

We can choose to be Jesus' helpers too.

Pray Together

Dear God, you have called us to be Jesus' helpers too. Show us what we can do. In Jesus' name. Amen.

At the Well

John 4:4-30, 39

CHOICE: Does the woman at the well tell her neighbors about Jesus? Or is the woman afraid to tell about Jesus?

Jesus now had twelve helpers. They followed him wherever he went.

One time Jesus and his helpers were traveling in another country. Jesus sat down by a well outside of a little town. While Jesus rested, the disciples went into town to get food.

Jesus had been walking all morning, and he was thirsty. He didn't have a cup with him to get water out of the well.

Then a woman came to get water. It was unusual to come for water in the middle of the day when it was hot. But she didn't want to be at the well when the other women came. She had done some things that she was ashamed of. So she didn't want to see other people. But Jesus was a stranger. He wouldn't know what she had done. She didn't need to hide from him.

Jesus asked her for a drink. She said, "Why are you asking me? Your people don't like my people."

Jesus told the woman that she didn't know who he was. If she did, she would ask *him* for help. Then she would never need help again.

Then Jesus said, "Go get your husband and bring him here."

The woman said, "I have no husband."

Jesus said, "That's right. You have had many husbands. And now you live with a man who is not your husband."

The woman was amazed. Jesus knew all about the things she had done. But he was the kindest man she had ever met. She knew he was special.

Jesus and the woman talked about worshiping God. Jesus told her that he was God's Son, the Savior of the world.

Just then the disciples came back to the well. But

they didn't ask what Jesus and the woman had been talking about.

The woman had a big choice to make. She could tell all her neighbors about Jesus. Of course, that meant facing people she did not want to see because she was ashamed. Or she could go home without saying anything about Jesus.

What did the woman do? She ran back to town. She was not afraid to face people now. Jesus cared about her. He had told her how to worship God.

The woman said to everyone, "Come meet a man who knows everything about me. He must be the Savior."

Many people came to listen to Jesus, even in the middle of a hot day. They were glad he had come to their town. They were glad that the woman had told them all about him.

God was happy too. The whole town found out about Jesus because the woman told them the wonderful news. That's how people learn about Jesus: Someone has to tell them!

Remember Together

What did Jesus ask a woman to give him?

Why did the woman not want to see other people?

Why did the woman decide to talk to her neighbors?

Did the woman make a good choice or a bad choice?

Think about YOUR Choices

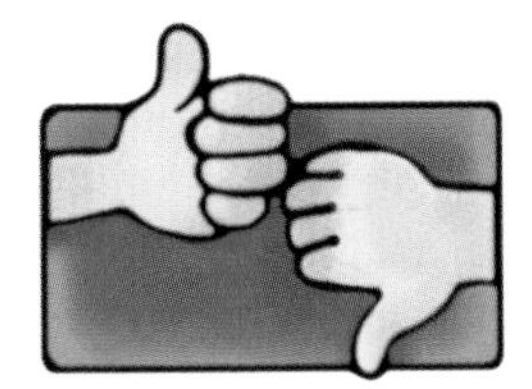

What can you tell your neighbors about Jesus? Can you play for them some of your favorite songs about Jesus? Can you tell about some of the pictures in your Bible storybooks?

Do a Good-Choice Activity

As you look at books, magazines, and catalogs, find different kinds of people. God loves them all! How can we choose to show love to others?

Jesus wants us to tell our neighbors what we know about him.

Pray Together

Dear God, thank you for loving us even though you know all about us. Show us ways that we can share that good news with our neighbors. In Jesus' name. Amen.

Long-Distance Healing

Matthew 8:5-13

CHOICE: Does a Roman army leader trust Jesus' power from a distance? Or does he think Jesus has to be right there?

Everywhere Jesus went, he told people about God's love. He also made sick people well just by touching them.

People heard about Jesus' power and love. So they came to see Jesus to be made well. They came from far away. They came to whatever town Jesus was in. Many times he could hardly move because of the huge crowd around him.

One day a Roman army leader came to see Jesus.

The leader had a helper at his house. He cared about his helper a great deal. This helper was sick, and no one could make him better. He was too sick to be moved to the place where Jesus was. So the army leader went to the place where Jesus was. The leader had probably heard many stories about Jesus making people well. Jesus usually asked what the sick people wanted. Then he touched them and made them well.

The man said to Jesus, "I have a sick helper at my house. He is in bed and can't move. He hurts all over."

Jesus said, "I will go to your house. I will make your helper well."

Now the Roman army leader had a big choice to make. He could let Jesus leave the crowd of people he was helping. He could let Jesus go with him to his house just as Jesus had promised that he would. Maybe it would not be too late for the helper to be healed. Or he could trust Jesus to make the helper well without even going to the house.

This is what the Roman army leader said to Jesus. "I am not good enough to have you come to my house. If you just say that my helper will be well, I know that

he will be. I know because I am an army leader. When I tell men to march, they march. I believe that you have power to make people well. If you say that my helper will be well, it will happen."

Jesus said, "What great faith you have! Go. Your helper is well!"

The army leader went back to his house as fast as he

could. There was his helper, all ready to work again. He was no longer sick! He got well right at the time Jesus said it would happen!

Jesus was glad that the army leader had so much faith in his power. He was glad that he could make the man's helper well again.

Remember Together

What did the Roman army leader believe Jesus could do?

Did the army leader make a good choice or a bad choice?

What happened to the helper?

Think about YOUR Choices

We can't see Jesus today. But we can still believe in his power. Who needs Jesus' help? Will you believe that he can help—even if he doesn't do it right away?

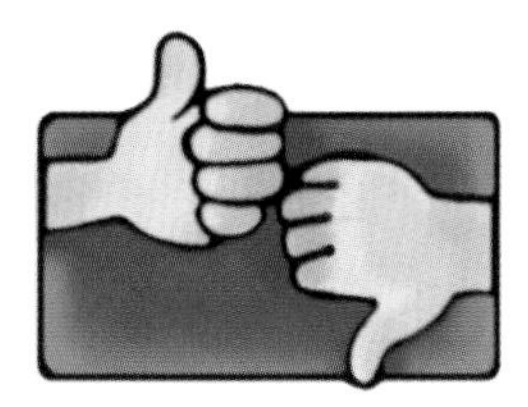

Do a Good-Choice Activity

Play a long-distance game. From another room, call out directions: jump, march, make a funny face. Then call out "hug" and run to get one! After you get your hug, pray for someone far away who needs a "hug" from Jesus.

We can believe that Jesus has power to help people near and far away.

Pray Together

Dear God, keep all our family well and safe. Be with those we love who are close by and those who are far away. In Jesus' name. Amen.

A Helping Hand

Matthew 12:9-14

CHOICE: Does Jesus choose to be kind and helpful? Or does he follow laws that show no love or caring?

Jesus knew all of God's laws. And Jesus obeyed them all because he loved God, his heavenly Father. But people had made up other laws. Some of these laws were not fair or helpful. They were often used to trick people.

One day Jesus and his disciples were at a worship place called a synagogue. It was the day of rest. This was a day for people to praise God and thank him for all his gifts. That's just what Jesus and his disciples were doing.

At the synagogue, Jesus saw a man with a hand that he couldn't use. He could not write or work or even dress himself. Jesus wanted to help the man. But the laws that people had made said that he couldn't do it. Helping the man would be work, and no one should work on the day of rest.

Now Jesus had a big choice to make. Jesus knew that one way to please God, his Father, is to be kind and helpful to others. So Jesus could heal the man's hand. But he was right at the synagogue where people were worshiping God. That meant someone would certainly notice and not like it. Jesus' other choice was to wait and help the man another day. But if he waited, the man might be gone.

What did Jesus do? He talked to the leaders at the synagogue who wanted to stop him. Jesus asked the leaders, "What if you had a sheep that fell into a hole? You would pull it out of the hole on the day of rest, wouldn't you? People are more important than sheep. So it's right to help someone on the day of rest.

Jesus then told the man, "Stretch out your hand." Right away his hand was healed!

God was glad that Jesus healed the man. That was a good way for Jesus to praise his Father in heaven.

Remember Together

On what day did Jesus go to the synagogue?
What did Jesus want to do for someone?
Why didn't the leaders want Jesus to help?
Did Jesus make a good choice or a bad choice?

Think about YOUR Choices

Which day is a special day to worship God? You can show your love for God by going to church. Can you show love for God by helping someone too?

Do a Good-Choice Activity

Here is something to do the next time you're in the car going to church. Make plans to do something kind and helpful. Maybe you can visit an elderly person or make a card for someone who is sick.

We can praise God on his special day by being kind and helpful.

Pray Together

Dear God, show us kind and helpful things to do on your special day. We want to show that we love you. In Jesus' name. Amen.

"Me First!"

Mark 9:33-37

CHOICE: Do the disciples help one another? Or do they argue about who is the most important?

The disciples spent most of their time together. They ate together and traveled together. They were sort of like a big family. They listened to Jesus and helped others know about God's love. Most of the time they were good friends and cared for each other. But sometimes, like in most families, they forgot all the things Jesus had been teaching them. They forgot to share and be kind. Sometimes they forgot to love.

One day the disciples were talking together as they walked to the next town. Maybe they talked about the weather. Maybe they tried to remember the stories Jesus had told earlier that day. Suddenly, one of the disciples

Finally, Jesus asked his disciples to tell him what they had been talking about. None of the twelve men said anything. They were afraid that Jesus knew everything they had said. And he did!

Jesus said to his disciples, "I know you want to be important. But if you want to be important to me, you must help everyone."

He picked up a little child and said, "Each of you should be kind to children like this. If you are kind to a child, it's the same as if you're kind to me. And being kind to me is the same as being kind to God, my Father in heaven."

The disciples felt sad because they knew Jesus did not want them to argue. They knew he wanted them to help others and to put others first. They were even to help each other and little children.

God wanted the disciples to care for each other. But he did not stop loving them when they argued about who was best. God's Son, Jesus, forgave them and showed them how to be better helpers.

Remember Together

What did the disciples argue about?

Did the disciples make a good choice or a bad choice?

What did the disciples learn about being important to Jesus?

Think about YOUR Choices

Can you be important to Jesus? Who are some people you can help? Perhaps everyone in your family can work together to help someone. You can help each other, too!

Do a Good-Choice Activity

Make a chart for the refrigerator that says, "I'm Jesus' friend. I can help others by ______." Leave space to write words or draw pictures of ways to help others.

Helping other people is better than trying to act important.

Pray Together

Dear God, forgive us for thinking we are more important to you than anyone else is. You love us all the same and want us to help each other! Thank you. In Jesus' name. Amen.

Jesus Loves Children

Matthew 19:13-15

CHOICE: Do Jesus' disciples let the children come to Jesus? Or do the disciples try to keep the children away?

One beautiful spring day a man came running into town with wonderful news. Jesus was coming to town! He would be there that very day!

All the fathers in the town probably got very busy. They may have cleared the path of rocks and branches. Perhaps they made a comfortable place for Jesus to sit. Then they must have watched for Jesus to come.

All the mothers probably got very busy too. They may have packed lunches. Perhaps they gave all the children baths. Then they probably put on their best clothes. Everyone was excited to see Jesus.

Finally someone called out that Jesus was almost

there! Everyone ran outside and watched. As the families waited, the fathers and mothers must have talked to each other. Perhaps they talked about how nice it would be if Jesus would hold their children. He could bless them—even the little babies. Jesus always talked about loving everyone. Surely that included children and babies.

Jesus came and sat in a comfortable spot, where he talked all morning. People listened closely. Even the

children seemed to know that someone special had come to town. They probably wondered if Jesus could see them.

At lunchtime the mothers unpacked the lunches, and everyone ate out on the grass. Jesus' disciples sat down close to him and talked softly. They didn't want anyone else to bother Jesus.

Then some of the fathers and mothers picked up their children. They carried their children toward Jesus.

But Jesus' disciples saw the families coming. The

..isciples didn't want the children to bother Jesus. Children probably didn't seem very important to them.

Now the disciples had a big choice to make. They could let the children come to Jesus. Or they could send the families away and not even tell Jesus they came.

This is what the disciples did. They told the parents to not let their children bother Jesus. The disciples said that he had no time for children. They said that Jesus was busy and didn't want to see them.

The parents were very sad. Did Jesus really not like children?

But Jesus heard what the disciples said. He called out, "Bring the children to me. They are the most important people in my kingdom."

All the children ran to sit on his lap. He told stories especially for them. Then he blessed them all. He prayed for each one, right down to the littlest baby.

All of the children were very happy! All of the mothers and fathers were happy too.

Then the disciples knew that they had been wrong. Jesus would never be too busy for children. He would always love the children, and they would always love him.

Remember Together

Why did families want to see Jesus?
What did the disciples say to the parents?
Did the disciples make a good choice or a bad choice?
What did Jesus do when he saw the children?

Think about YOUR Choices

Have you ever treated people as if they weren't very special? Maybe you didn't listen to a little brother, a sister, or a neighbor. All people are special to Jesus, so they should be special to you, too!

Do a Good-Choice Activity

Look at this Bible storybook with some of the children you know. That will be just like taking them to Jesus!

Our friends should be special to us because they are special to Jesus.

Pray Together

Jesus, I'm glad that you love me and that all children are special to you. Help me show by the way I act that I think they are special too. In your name I pray. Amen.

Who Will Help?

Luke 10:25-37

CHOICE: Does a Samaritan man help someone who has been hurt? Or does he walk by?

"Who is my neighbor?"

A man asked Jesus that question one day. It was important for the man to know the answer. It was important because God's laws say, "Love God with all your heart. And love your neighbor as much as you love yourself."

To answer the man's question, Jesus told this story:

"A man was traveling on a lonely road. He had been

in the city of Jerusalem. Now he was on his way to the town of Jericho. He didn't know it, but robbers were waiting for him. Suddenly, there they were! They seemed to come out of nowhere. They beat him and took his money. Then they left him by the side of the road.

"A man who led the worship at the temple came down the road. He saw the man who was hurt, but he didn't know the man. And he didn't stop to help. Maybe he was in a hurry, or maybe he just didn't care.

"Someone else came down the road. He helped with the worship at the temple too. He saw the man who was hurt, but he didn't know who he was. And he didn't stop to help. Maybe he was busy, or maybe he thought he would get dirty.

"Then a stranger from Samaria came down the road. The stranger saw the man who was hurt. He didn't know who the man was, but he knew that the man needed help.

"Now the stranger had a big choice to make. He could stop and help the hurt man. Or he could go on his way like the others did.

"This is what the stranger did. He stopped his donkey and ran over to the man. He cleaned the man's hurt places and wrapped them in strips of cloth. He lifted the man onto his own donkey and slowly led him down the road. He took the man to an inn with rooms where travelers could stay. There he stayed all night and took care of the man."

"In the morning the stranger had to go on with his trip. But he gave money to the man who was in charge at the inn. He told him to take care of the man who was hurt. He said, 'If you need more money, I'll pay you when I return.' Then the stranger left."

That was the end of Jesus' story. Then Jesus asked, "Who was a good neighbor to the man hurt by robbers?"

The person who had been listening to Jesus' story knew the answer. He said, "The good neighbor was the stranger who stopped to help."

Jesus said, "You're right. Now go and be that kind of neighbor yourself."

Remember Together

What do God's laws say about loving our neighbors?

In Jesus' story, who needed help from a neighbor?

What did the stranger from Samaria do for the hurt man?

Did the stranger make a good choice or a bad choice?

Think about YOUR Choices

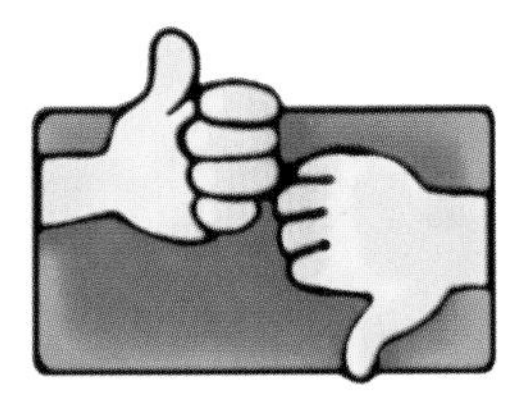

Some of our neighbors are people we know. What are some ways that we can help them? Some of our neighbors are strangers. What are good rules for staying safe when a stranger needs help?

Do a Good-Choice Activity

Make a list of numbers to call if someone near you is hurt or sick. Then practice making the calls with a toy phone.

God helps us know how to be good neighbors.

Pray Together

Dear God, thank you for good neighbors and for showing us ways to be good neighbors ourselves. In Jesus' name. Amen.

Far from Home

Luke 15:11-24

CHOICE: Does the Prodigal Son admit he was wrong and come home? Or does he think it's right to stay away?

When Jesus told a story, people wanted to listen. They understood the stories because they were about people like themselves.

One day Jesus told a story about a family. The family had a father and two sons. The older son helped his father on the farm. The younger son wanted to see the world. He wanted all of the money from the family that should belong to him someday. And he wanted it right now.

It was the son's right to choose when he would get his money. So his father gave it to him and said good-bye.

The young man went to a country far away. There he did many things that were wrong, and he spent all of his money.

When his money was gone, he couldn't buy any food. He was hungry. So he got a job feeding pigs. He was so hungry that the pigs' food looked good enough to eat!

Then the young son thought, *The men who work for my father have more food to eat than they need. And I have no food at all.*

Now the young son had a big choice to make. He could go home and ask his father to forgive him for the wrong things he had done. He could tell his father that he would work for his food. Or the young son could stay with the pigs. He could decide that he had done nothing wrong. And he could forget all about going back to his family.

What did the young son do? He jumped up and ran out of the pigpen. He ran all the way home.

His father was looking for him and saw him coming. He saw that his son was dirty and dressed in rags. Was the father angry? Was he upset? No! All he could think about was how much he loved his son. He was so glad that the young man had come home!

The father ran out to meet his son and hugged him. The young man told his father how sorry he was. He said, “I’m not good enough to be your son anymore.”

But do you know what the father did? He brought out the best clothes in the house for his son. Then he asked his helpers to get a big dinner ready. And he

invited everyone to come and see his son who had come home.

Jesus told this story to help people. He wanted them to know that God is like the father in the story.

He told the story for people who are like the young son. People who do things that are wrong can be sorry. They can come back to God's family. And God will always welcome them back home again.

Remember Together

Why did the young son in Jesus' story wish he had some of the pigs' food?

When he decided to go home, did the son make a good choice or a bad choice?

How did the father greet him when he came home?

Who is like the father in the story?

Think about YOUR Choices

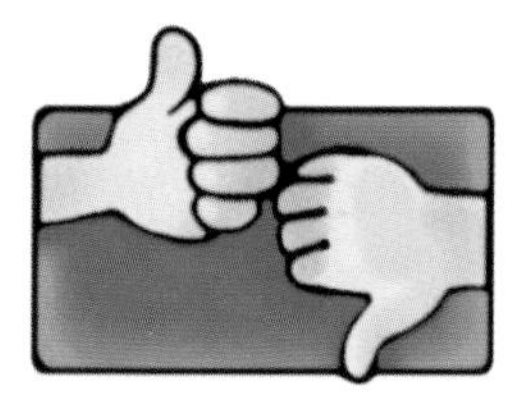

Is it hard to say you're sorry? How can members of your family show forgiveness to one another? Can you hug each other? Can you talk to God together?

Do a Good-Choice Activity

Play hide-and-seek. Each time someone is found, hug and run for home.

We can talk to God about wrong things we've done, and he will still love us.

Pray Together

Dear God, help us to say we're sorry whenever we need to. Thank you for being such a loving father. In Jesus' name. Amen.

Look Everywhere

Matthew 18:12-14; Luke 15:3-7; John 10:11

CHOICE: Does a shepherd keep looking for his lost lamb? Or does he give up?

Another story Jesus told was about a shepherd who had a lot of sheep. He had more than 20 sheep. He had more than 50 sheep. He had 100 sheep!

Every day the shepherd took his sheep out to the field. There they ate green grass and drank cool water. They played in the sun and took naps in the shade.

Every evening the shepherd brought his sheep home to the sheep pen. He counted them to make sure they were all there—97, 98, 99, 100. All there. So he closed the gate, and they were safe for the night.

One night the shepherd was counting his sheep—97, 98, 99 . . . What? Where was number 100! Where was the last little sheep? She was lost! Maybe she was in a thornbush or between some rocks or in a cave. Maybe she was hurt.

Now the shepherd had a big choice to make. He could go out into the dark and look for the little lost sheep. He could keep looking until he found her. Or the shepherd could stay home. After all, he had 99 other sheep that were safe in the pen. And maybe the lost sheep didn't want to be in the pen anyway.

What did the shepherd do? He made sure that the sheep in the sheep pen were safe. Then he probably put on his coat. He took his shepherd's stick and went back out to look for his little lost sheep.

He looked high up in the hills. No little sheep.

He looked in the rocky caves. No little sheep.

He looked by the stream of water. No little sheep.

Finally he walked toward the thornbushes on the far side of the field. He thought he heard a little

sound: *Baa. Baa.* He ran over to the bushes, and there was the little sheep!

The good shepherd took her in his arms and held her close. He lifted her up onto his shoulders and carried her all the way home.

When he got home, the shepherd called all his friends. He said, "Come and be happy with me! My little sheep was lost, and I have found her."

All the sheep in the pen were glad to have the little sheep home again. They were glad that the shepherd cared for each one of them.

Jesus called himself the Good Shepherd. He loves each one of us just like the shepherd loved his little lost sheep.

Jesus doesn't want anyone to be lost. He wants everyone to follow him. Jesus, the Good Shepherd, can help everyone to be safe in God's family.

Remember Together

How many sheep did the shepherd have?

What did the shepherd learn when he counted his sheep one night?

Did the shepherd make a good choice or a bad choice?

How did the shepherd feel when he found his little lost sheep?

Who is like the kind shepherd?

Think about YOUR Choices

Jesus is your shepherd. How can you follow him? How can you learn to love and obey him?

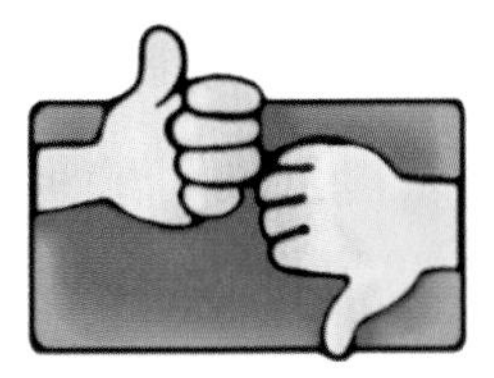

Do a Good-Choice Activity

Play hide-and-seek just as you did after the last story. This time, pretend that you're a little lost sheep. Say *baa* softly to help your shepherd find you.

We can follow Jesus, our Good Shepherd, by learning to love and obey him.

Pray Together

Dear God, thank you for sending Jesus to be our Good Shepherd. We want to be safe in your family forever. In Jesus' name. Amen.

"Thank You, Jesus!"

Luke 17:11-19

CHOICE: Does a man thank Jesus for making him well? Or does he run off with his nine friends?

Jesus often walked from place to place. He met many people. They wanted to hear about God's love for each of them.

Some people who wanted to see Jesus were sick. They had heard that Jesus could make sick people well.

One day Jesus met ten men who were sick with leprosy. The law said that people with leprosy couldn't live near anyone else. If they did, other

people might get leprosy too. So these men had to live far away from their families. It was the law.

The ten men saw Jesus coming down the road. They stayed far away from Jesus because they knew what the law said. They knew that they could not get close to anyone. But they wanted Jesus to make them well. So they called out to Jesus, using their loudest voices. They shouted, "Jesus, please help us!"

Jesus knew what the men wanted. He said, "Go home. You won't be sick anymore."

The ten men started to run for home. How happy they would be to see their families! As they were running, they looked at themselves. They saw that their sores were gone!

Nine of the men kept running, but one man stopped. He knew that Jesus had done a wonderful thing for him.

Now the man who stopped had a big choice to make. He could go back and say thank you to Jesus. He knew that would be the right thing to do. Or he could keep running with the other nine men. Why should he stop if they didn't? He wanted to get home just as much as they did.

This is what the one man did. He decided that it would be wrong to go even one step farther. First he had to go back and thank Jesus. So the man turned around and ran back to where Jesus was standing. He threw himself on the ground and thanked Jesus over and over for making him well. He praised God for his healing power.

Jesus said, "Weren't there ten sick men? Where are the other nine that I made well? Only you have come to thank me."

The man knew that the others had gone home. But he didn't say anything. He was just glad that he had chosen to come back and thank Jesus.

Jesus smiled at the man. He said, "You can get up now and go home to your family. You believed that I could help you, and now you are well."

So the man ran home. When he got there, his family was so happy to see him. He was happy to see them, too. And how glad he was that he had met Jesus!

Remember Together

How many men were sick?
How did Jesus help them?
Why did one man stop?
Did the man make a good choice or a bad choice?

Think about YOUR Choices

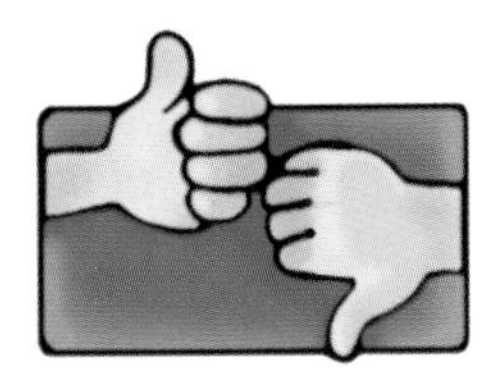

When someone helps you, what do you say?
How does God help you? What do you say?

Do a Good-Choice Activity

God gives us many gifts—friends, family, food, clothes, animals, healthy bodies, etc. See if you can think of one gift for each letter of the alphabet. You may want to send a thank-you prayer to God for one of these gifts every day.

Choosing to thank God makes everyone happy!

Pray Together

Dear God, thank you for being with us when we are sick. Thank you for all the good days when we are well. Help us to be thankful for everything you do. In Jesus' name. Amen.

See the Birds

Mark 10:46-52

CHOICE: Does Bartimaeus trust Jesus to help him? Or doesn't he try to talk to Jesus?

Bartimaeus liked to be outdoors. He could feel the soft wind on his face. He could hear the birds sing. He could smell bread baking.

But Bartimaeus was blind, so he couldn't see. He couldn't see anything at all.

All day Bartimaeus sat by the road begging. Whenever someone walked past him, he would ask that person for money. It was the only way he could get money to buy food. Some people gave him a little. Some people gave him a lot. Some gave nothing at all.

Then Bartimaeus got a wonderful gift. He heard about Jesus. He heard that Jesus could help people, even people who had never been able to see.

Bartimaeus must have wondered who Jesus was. Could this man really help him see?

One day Bartimaeus sat down by the road, just as he always did. But something was different on this day. Bartimaeus used his ears to listen carefully. He heard a crowd of people gathering near the road. They were talking about Jesus. He was coming down the road this very day! The people in the crowd began to cheer. Jesus was on the road near Bartimaeus!

Now Bartimaeus had a big choice to make. He could shout over the crowd and hope to meet Jesus. He could believe that Jesus would be able to help him. Maybe Jesus could even help him see. Or Bartimaeus could just keep begging by the side of the road. With this big crowd, he could get quite a bit of money today. Besides, he didn't really know if Jesus could help him.

What did Bartimaeus do? He shouted, "Jesus, help me!"

But the crowd was big and noisy. No one wanted Bartimaeus to get in the way. So the people near him told him to be quiet.

Bartimaeus wouldn't be quiet. He shouted again, "Jesus, please help me!"

Jesus stopped and told some people to bring Bartimaeus to him. "Come," someone said to the man who was blind. "Jesus wants to see you."

What wonderful news! Bartimaeus jumped up and threw his coat to one side. Before he knew it, Bartimaeus was standing in front of Jesus. Jesus said, "What do you want?"

Bartimaeus said, "I want to see."

Jesus smiled. He said, "You believed that I could help you, and now you can see." Bartimaeus slowly opened his eyes. And, yes, he could see! Probably the first thing he saw was Jesus' smile! Then he saw birds and clouds and the road. And he saw all the people in the crowd.

Bartimaeus followed Jesus down the road. Now he could see where he was going! He was so glad that he had called out to Jesus. And Jesus was glad that Bartimaeus had trusted him to help.

Remember Together

What did Bartimaeus want Jesus to do for him?

Did Bartimaeus make a good choice or a bad choice?

How did Jesus help Bartimaeus?

Who was happy then?

Think about YOUR Choices

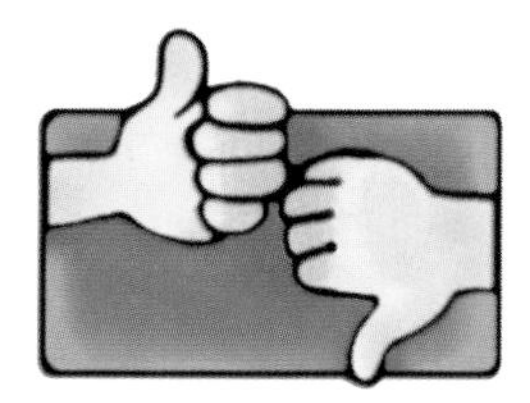

Is there something you would like Jesus to do for you or for a friend? Jesus can always make people well, but sometimes he helps in different ways. How might Jesus help someone if he doesn't make the person well? How can you help someone who can't see, hear, or walk as well as you can?

Do a Good-Choice Activity

Set a timer for several times during one day. Thank God for all the things you can see (or hear or touch) each time the timer goes off.

We can trust God to help us take care of our body.

Pray Together

Dear God, thank you for our eyes and ears and everything! Help us choose to take good care of our body. In Jesus' name. Amen.

"Come Sit with Me"

Luke 10:38-42

CHOICE: Does Mary listen to Jesus? Or is she too busy?

In the little town of Bethany some women were bringing water home from the well. Some women were grinding flour for bread. Some women were washing the clothes. But in one little house, two sisters were probably doing all of those things. They must have been dusting and baking and putting things in place, too. Mary and Martha were getting ready for a visit from their friend Jesus!

Soon the house was clean, and the food was cooking.

Then Jesus came. Mary and Martha were his special friends, so Jesus was always happy to visit them. He sat down to talk with them about God's love.

Martha thought about all of the things that still needed to be done. Perhaps she had to see if the food was ready yet. Then everything would have to be dished up in bowls. And Jesus would want something to drink. Martha needed Mary to help her.

Now Mary had a big choice to make. She could sit and listen to Jesus talk about God's love. Jesus was such a good teacher. She loved to listen to him. Or Mary could help Martha. She could let Jesus sit and wait while she was busy working.

What did Mary do? She sat down right by Jesus' feet. She wanted to be sure that she could hear everything he said. Jesus smiled to see her listening so carefully.

But Martha didn't smile at all. She said to Jesus, "I'm doing all of the work by myself. Tell Mary to help me."

Jesus said, "Martha, Martha. Don't be upset. Mary wants to hear about God's love. That's what is most important."

Jesus had so many stories to tell, and he could stay for just a little while. How he wished that Martha would also come and sit with him. He wanted her to hear about God's love too.

Remember Together

Why were Martha and Mary so busy?

What did Jesus want to do when he came to visit?

What did Martha want Mary to do?

Did Mary make a good choice or a bad choice?

Think about YOUR Choices

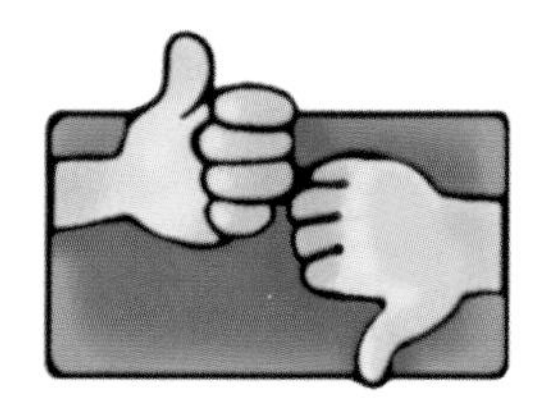

Are you a good listener? How can you learn to be a better listener? Name ways you can hear about God's love. (Listen to someone read Bible stories; watch Bible videos and television programs; listen to songs about Jesus; etc.)

Do a Good-Choice Activity

Find someone who likes to talk about God, and ask that person to tell you about God's love. It might be a parent, grandparent, neighbor, Sunday school teacher, pastor, etc. Be sure to listen carefully!

God is pleased when we listen to people who tell about his love.

Pray Together

Dear God, help us choose to be good listeners when someone is talking about you or your Son, Jesus. Amen.

Up a Tree

Luke 19:1-10

CHOICE: Does Zacchaeus tell Jesus that he is sorry and start doing what's right? Or does he keep doing wrong things?

Zacchaeus was a little man who lived in a little town. He was a rich man, but he was not happy. He got his money by cheating people. He took more tax money from them than he should have. He kept the extra for himself. People didn't like the way Zacchaeus cheated, so they wouldn't be his friends. He was all alone.

One day Zacchaeus found out that Jesus was coming to town. At first Zacchaeus probably didn't care. He wasn't sick, and he could see. So he didn't need Jesus' help. But then he may have thought about Jesus wanting to be everyone's friend. Maybe he should at least try to see what Jesus was like.

So Zacchaeus went to the road where Jesus would be coming. But everyone else in town did that too! There were so many people that Zacchaeus couldn't see anything. He was too short. And since no one liked him, he probably didn't even ask if he could stand in front.

Then Zacchaeus had a good idea. He climbed up into a tree by the street where Jesus would be walking. He sat on a branch behind some leaves. Now he could see everything, but he didn't think anyone could see him!

Jesus came closer and closer. Zacchaeus saw that he looked kind, but would he be a friend to someone who cheats? Jesus walked closer and closer until . . . stop! Jesus stopped right under the tree where Zacchaeus was! He looked up into the branches and saw Zacchaeus. Jesus said, "Zacchaeus, come down. I'm coming home with you today."

Zacchaeus could hardly believe it. Only a friend would come to his house. Jesus wanted to be his friend. But what about the money that Zacchaeus had gotten by cheating?

Now Zacchaeus had a big choice to make. He could

climb down and let Jesus come home with him. Jesus and he could become friends. Or Zacchaeus could wait for Jesus to go away. Then Zacchaeus would still be a rich man with a nice house.

What did Zacchaeus do? He came down as quick as a squirrel. He led Jesus home to his house, and they talked together.

Being with Jesus made Zacchaeus feel sorry about the

wrong things he had done. He said, "I'm going to give half of my things to poor people. And if I've taken too much money for taxes, I'll pay the people back four times as much as I took from them." Jesus' friendship was worth all the money Zacchaeus would give back.

Jesus was glad that Zacchaeus was sorry about the wrong things he had done. Jesus was glad that Zacchaeus finally wanted to do what was right. He said to Zacchaeus, "I came to find and to help people like you. Now you are safe in God's family."

Remember Together

How did Zacchaeus get his money?
Why did he climb a tree?
What did Jesus say to Zacchaeus?
Did Zacchaeus make a good choice or a bad choice?
How was Zacchaeus different after Jesus came to visit him?

Think about YOUR Choices

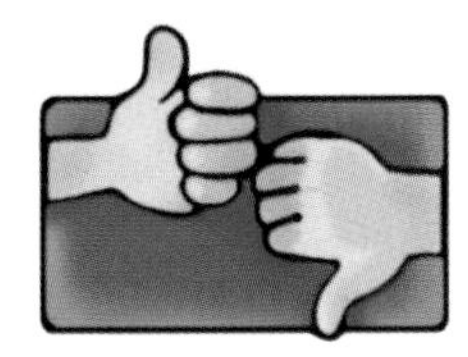

Jesus wants to be your friend. What wrong things can he help you stop doing?

Do a Good-Choice Activity

Crawl under a table and watch feet passing by. Then stand on a chair and look at the world from up high like Zacchaeus did. Set an extra plate for dinner and talk to Jesus as if he were right there. (He really is, you know!)

We can ask Jesus to help us stop doing wrong things and start doing what's right!

Pray Together

Dear God, it's good to know that Jesus wants to be our friend forever. We're sorry about ________, and now we want to do what's right. In Jesus' name. Amen.

A Gift for Jesus

Luke 7:36-50

CHOICE: Does a woman give Jesus a special gift? Or does she keep it for herself?

Jesus enjoyed eating dinner with friends. They could talk and laugh and relax together.

One day an important man named Simon invited Jesus to come to his house for dinner. Many people had been invited. But one woman there probably had not been invited. This woman had done some things that she was ashamed of. Everyone knew about the wrong things she had done. And most people didn't like her.

But the woman had heard Jesus talk about God's love. She was sure that Jesus cared about her. So she wanted to give Jesus a wonderful gift, the best thing she owned. It was a jar of wonderful-smelling oils. She knew that Jesus' feet were hot and dry from walking all day in his sandals. The oil would feel so good on his dry feet.

Now the woman had a big choice to make. She could pour out the wonderful oils on Jesus' feet. That would be one way to thank him for caring about her. It would be one way to thank him for his wonderful news of God's forgiveness. Or the woman could leave quietly with her jar of oils. Maybe Jesus would not want her to touch him. Maybe he didn't really care about her.

What did the woman do? She poured the oils on Jesus' feet and began to rub them in. Then she wiped his feet with her long hair. As the wonderful smell of the oils filled the room, many of the dinner guests probably looked around and saw her.

Simon, the important man who had invited the people to his house, saw the woman. He knew the kind of life she had lived. So he told Jesus who she was. And he said that she had done wrong things.

Jesus said to Simon, "You didn't do anything to welcome me when I came to your house. You didn't wash my feet or greet me. But this woman has shown me how much she loves me."

Then Jesus looked at the woman. And she looked right into Jesus' face. She saw how much he loved her. Yes, Jesus knew who she was and what she had done. He also knew that she wanted to change and live differently. He knew she had heard about God's love and forgiveness.

The woman began to cry. But she wasn't sad. The tears she cried were happy tears. She was glad that Jesus understood her. And she was glad that he loved her so much.

Jesus said to the woman, "Your sins are forgiven. You have believed in me, and now you will be safe in God's family. Go in peace."

How glad the woman was that she had given her gift to Jesus. And how glad Jesus was that he was able to forgive her sins.

Remember Together

Why did a woman want to put oil on Jesus' feet?
Did she make a good choice or a bad choice?
What did Jesus say to the woman after she gave him her gift?

Think about YOUR Choices

What is the best gift you ever gave someone? Why did you want that person to have something so wonderful? You can give gifts to Jesus, too. Jesus says that giving gifts to other people is the same as giving him gifts! And when you tell him that you love him or that you're sorry about wrong things you've done, that's a gift.

Do a Good-Choice Activity

Draw a picture of a jar and dab perfume on it. Give it as a gift to someone to show that you love Jesus.

Giving gifts to others is one way to show that we love Jesus.

Pray Together

Dear Jesus, we love you. Help us to show our love for you by doing what's right. In your name. Amen.

Into Jerusalem

Matthew 21:1-11, 14-16; Luke 19:29-40

CHOICE: Do Jesus' disciples get a donkey for him? Or do they decide it would be better not to help Jesus ride into Jerusalem?

Jesus was standing on a hill near the city of Jerusalem. He had been traveling around the country for about three years. Everywhere he went, there were crowds of people. They wanted to hear all about God's love for them. The sick people wanted Jesus to make them well. Those who had done wrong things wanted Jesus to forgive them. Lots of people liked what Jesus said and did. Some of the people even wanted to make Jesus their king.

But in Jerusalem, many of the leaders did not like Jesus. They were afraid that if Jesus was the king, they would not be so powerful anymore. So they had tried to trick him with hard questions, but Jesus always knew just what to say. They had tried to catch him breaking the laws, but Jesus did just the right things. Finally the men went back to Jerusalem to wait and think some more. Somehow they had to get rid of Jesus.

Jesus knew that sad things were going to happen to him. But he also knew that it was time to go into Jerusalem. So on a hill near the city, Jesus talked to two of his helpers. He said, "I want you to go into the little town near Jerusalem. You'll find a young donkey tied up there. No one has ever ridden on this little donkey. Bring it to me. If anyone asks what you're doing, say that I need the donkey."

Now Jesus' helpers had a big choice to make. They could find the donkey and bring it to Jesus just as he asked them to do. Or they could pretend that they couldn't find the donkey. They could try to keep Jesus from going into Jerusalem. After all, it probably wouldn't be safe to go there.

What did Jesus' helpers do? They went into town and found the donkey. They told the owner, "Jesus

needs it." Then they brought the donkey to Jesus and put their coats on its back. They wanted Jesus to have something soft to sit on.

Sitting on the donkey's back, Jesus rode down the big hill toward Jerusalem. People cheered and shouted, "Hosanna! Jesus is our king!" They laid their coats down on the road. And they waved palm branches.

Jesus was glad to see the people. And he was glad

that his helpers had brought him the little donkey. When he got into the city, he made sick people well. He listened to the happy shouts of the children, too.

But Jesus was sad, too. He saw the leaders who didn't like him. And he knew that soon he would have to face them. But that was OK, because that's why he had come.

Remember Together

What was the name of the city where Jesus was going?

What did Jesus ask two of his helpers to do?

Did the helpers make a good choice or a bad choice?

How did the people welcome Jesus?

Why was Jesus sad?

Think about YOUR Choices

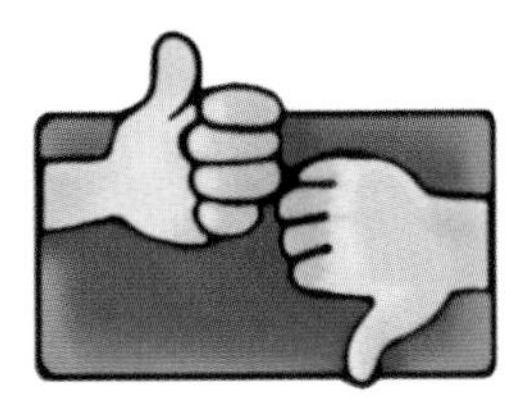

Did you ever have to do something but you didn't understand why you had to do it? How can you know if something is right to do? (It's right if it's something God says to do, such as being kind, trusting, obeying parents and teachers, etc.)

Do a Good-Choice Activity

Act out the Bible story, pretending to be Jesus' helpers. You'll look for a donkey, put your coat on the donkey, wave palm branches, and cheer for Jesus. But you'll wonder why Jesus wants to go into Jerusalem, where some people don't like him.

We should obey God even when we don't know why he wants us to do something.

Pray Together

Dear God, we want to do what's right even when we don't understand everything. In Jesus' name we pray. Amen.

Just Two Small Coins

Luke 21:1-4

CHOICE: Does a poor woman give her money for God's work? Or does she keep it for herself?

As Jesus sat at the Temple, he watched people come and go. Some were old. Some were young. Some were rich. They wore fancy robes and had rings on their fingers. Some were poor. They wore old clothes and had no rings for their fingers. But people wanted to come to the Temple to praise God.

People also wanted to give money for God's work. There was a jar just for collecting the money. Jesus sat near it one day. His helpers were with him.

Jesus and his helpers watched as some rich people came to the offering jar. They all had many coins in their money bags. They took a lot of coins out of their

bags and put the money in the offering jar. But they still had a lot of money left.

The rich people probably looked around to see if anyone was watching. Then they dropped their big coins into the jar: one, two, three, four, five, six, seven, eight, nine, ten! Everyone must have smiled to see the rich people give so much money. The rich people smiled too. They still had a lot of money in their bags. So giving a lot had cost them just a little.

Then Jesus and his helpers saw a poor woman come in. She was all alone and wore old clothes. She reached into her money bag and counted her coins: one, two. Two small coins were all she had.

Now the poor woman had a big choice to make. She could put her two small coins into the offering for God's work. Then she could trust God to take care of her. Or she could keep the money she had and spend it later on something that she needed.

This is what the woman did. She went over to the offering jar without looking around like the rich people did. She wasn't expecting anyone to watch. Quietly she put the two small coins in the jar.

But someone *was* watching. It was Jesus! He talked to his helpers about the gift that the poor woman gave to God. Jesus said that her little gift was much better than the big gifts from the rich people.

Why did Jesus say that? Jesus told his helpers that the rich people gave just a little of their money. But the woman loved God so much that she gave everything she had. That was the best gift.

God was pleased that the woman wanted to give what she had for his work. God took good care of her. The woman must have been glad that she had used her money to help with God's work. Surely she knew that she had done the right thing, and that made her very happy.

Remember Together

Why was there an offering jar at the Temple?

When the rich people gave money, what was left in their money bags?

When the poor woman gave money, what did she have left?

Did the woman make a good choice or a bad choice?

Why was the woman's gift the best gift?

Think about YOUR Choices

What are some things that you like to buy with your money? Do you make sure that there is money for God's work first? What other gifts can you give to God besides money?

Do a Good-Choice Activity

Plan a way to earn money, such as recycling, doing yard work, or helping with extra chores. Choose to give all of the money to help with God's work—church, missions, food pantry, etc. How does that feel?

God is pleased when we give what we can for his work.

Pray Together

Dear God, help us choose to give generously because you have given us so much! In Jesus' name. Amen.

Who Is the Servant?

Luke 22:7-13; John 13:1-17

CHOICE: Does Jesus help others? Or does he ask others to help him?

All week long, Jesus taught at the Temple or in the streets. Huge crowds came to hear him. Some of the people wanted him to be the king. But some of the leaders did not like Jesus. They were making plans to get rid of him.

One day Jesus had two of his helpers, Peter and John, get a room ready. It was a room upstairs in a house. Jesus wanted to eat a special dinner just with his helpers,

the disciples. This was a special feast to remember Moses and the trip out of Egypt. Everyone would eat and talk and remember the stories about Moses.

At sunset Jesus and his helpers gathered around a table in the room upstairs. They were probably all tired and hungry, so they sat down to eat right away. While they were eating, Jesus saw a bowl and a clean towel. These were for washing everyone's feet.

In Bible times people always wore sandals. So their

feet got hot and dirty from walking on the dusty roads. But washing feet was a job for servants, not for teachers and leaders. Jesus knew that.

Now Jesus had a big choice to make. He could show his disciples how to help others by washing their feet for them. Then they would understand that he came to help them. And they would know that he wanted them to help one another. Or Jesus could let the servants wash everyone's feet as usual. Maybe he could just talk about helping others. And he could tell his disciples that they should be good helpers.

What did Jesus do? He took off his robe and sandals. Then he filled the bowl with water. And he wrapped the big towel around himself. He got down on his knees by one of his helpers and washed his feet. One after another, he washed his disciples' feet.

Then he came to Peter, who said, "No! You can't wash my feet." Peter didn't think it was right for Jesus to be working like that. After all, he was the disciples' teacher.

But Jesus said to Peter, "If you want to be my helper, you must first let me help you." Even Peter let Jesus wash his feet then.

When Jesus was finished, he put his robe on again and sat at the table. He said, "Now you have seen what it is like to help others. I have been like a servant to you. I didn't help you because I had to. I did it because I love you and I want to help you. You must do what I've done. Help each other and other people too."

God was glad that Jesus showed his disciples how to help others. God knew that the disciples would be happy when they helped others.

Remember Together

Why were the disciples eating a special meal?

What did Jesus do to help his disciples?

Did Jesus make a good choice or a bad choice?

Why didn't Peter want his feet washed?

What did Jesus teach his disciples about helping?

Think about YOUR Choices

What are some of the ways that you help at home? at school? at church? Is helping sometimes hard work? Who are you like when you help others?

Do a Good-Choice Activity

Our feet may not get so dusty, but our hands always get dirty. Ask your family if you can take turns washing each other's hands.

Helping others makes everyone happy!

Pray Together

Dear God, we're glad for all the ways that you help us. Show us the best ways to help others. In Jesus' name. Amen.

"Wake Up!"

Mark 14:26, 32-42

CHOICE: Are the disciples faithful friends in the garden? Or do they fall asleep instead of praying for Jesus?

After Jesus and his helpers ate dinner together, they sang a song. Then they went downstairs and began walking to the Garden of Gethsemane. Jesus wanted to go there because it was a quiet place to pray. Jesus knew that what he soon had to face was going to be very hard. He wanted to talk to God about it. And he wanted his best friends to be with him.

They all walked to the Garden together. Jesus had told his disciples several times what was going to happen. But they didn't believe that anyone would hurt Jesus. They would never let that happen.

Jesus left most of the disciples near the entrance to the garden. He took Peter, James, and John with him a little farther into the garden. They were his three best friends. He said to them, "I'm so very, very sad. Stay here and keep watch while I go still a little farther to pray."

The three disciples must have known that it was important for them to stay awake. It was important for them to pray while Jesus prayed.

Now the disciples had a big choice to make. They could try to stay awake and keep watch as Jesus had asked them to do. They could pray even though they didn't know just what sad things were going to happen. Or Jesus' helpers could close their eyes for just a minute. They had eaten a big dinner, and it was late at night. And really, what bad things could happen in the garden?

This is what they did. Soon all of the disciples, even Peter and James and John, were sound asleep.

While they slept, Jesus talked to God, his father in heaven. He prayed, "If it's possible, take away the sad things that are ahead of me. But it's not what I want that's important. I'll do whatever you want me to do."

Jesus checked on his disciples two times. But they were sleeping each time. "Are you sleeping?" asked Jesus. "Can't you stay awake and pray?"

The third time Jesus came back, Jesus' helpers really woke up. It was not morning, but a huge crowd was coming toward them. The men had torches of fire, sharp swords, and big sticks. They were looking for

Jesus. They marched right past the disciples, who suddenly weren't sleepy anymore. It was the start of a long night with no more sleep.

God was sorry that the disciples had not stayed awake to pray. He wished that they had done what his Son, Jesus, had asked them to do. But God was with Jesus' helpers as the men took Jesus away. And all through the night God was with Jesus, too.

Remember Together

Where did the disciples go after dinner?

What did Jesus want to do there?

Who went farther into the Garden with him?

What did Jesus ask them to do?

Did the disciples make a good choice or a bad choice?

Think about YOUR Choices

Who can you really count on when you need help? Can others count on you like that? Can Jesus count on you to do what he asks?

Do a Good-Choice Activity

Ask Jesus to help you plan something special to do for him. Then try to do it every day for a week. Maybe you'll tell Jesus how much you love him. Maybe you'll do something kind for one of Jesus' friends. Be sure to do what you planned before you go to sleep each night!

We should never get tired of doing what Jesus wants us to do.

Pray Together

Dear God, help us to never give up doing the things Jesus wants us to do. In Jesus' name we pray. Amen.

By the Fire

Luke 22:54-62; John 13:37-38; 18:10-11, 15-18, 25-27

CHOICE: Is Peter brave enough to be Jesus' friend? Or does Peter pretend he doesn't know Jesus?

Peter was a good disciple. He listened to Jesus and learned from him. He loved Jesus very much.

Jesus knew that Peter loved him, but he also knew that Peter wasn't very brave. Just after Jesus and his helpers ate their special dinner together, Jesus talked to Peter. Jesus said, "Before the rooster crows you'll say three times that you don't know me."

Peter was shocked. He said, "No! I would never do that." Peter thought he was brave. He would never pretend that he didn't know his best friend.

Then men came to the Garden with their torches of fire, sharp swords, and big sticks. Peter tried to be brave by using his sharp sword to hurt one of the men. But that's not what Jesus wanted Peter to do.

All of the disciples left. Later Peter wanted to be near Jesus to see what was going on. So he came to the closed-in yard near the place where Jesus was.

It was a cool night, and there was a fire out in the yard. People stood by the fire talking quietly. So Peter walked over to the fire to warm himself.

Suddenly a serving girl said to him, "You're not one of Jesus' helpers, are you?"

Now Peter had a big choice to make. He could let the girl and everyone else know that he was Jesus' helper. But then he might get in trouble. Someone might try to hurt him. Or Peter could say that he wasn't Jesus' helper. Then he would be safe. And perhaps Jesus would never find out that he lied.

This is what Peter did. He was afraid, so he told a lie. He said, "No, I'm not Jesus' helper." He went back to warming himself by the fire.

Later someone else said to him, "Aren't you one of Jesus' disciples?"

But once again Peter said, "No. I am not one of Jesus' disciples."

Then a man said, "I'm sure I saw you with Jesus."

And a third time Peter said, "No! I don't know the man at all." At that moment a rooster crowed.

Peter suddenly remembered Jesus' words. Just as Jesus had said, Peter pretended three times that he didn't know Jesus.

Then Jesus looked right at Peter, who couldn't have felt any worse. Peter hid his face in his robe and ran away from the place where Jesus was. He cried and cried.

Jesus was sad too, but he knew that someday he would talk to Peter again. Then Peter would know how much Jesus still loved him. And Peter would learn to be very brave.

Remember Together

What did Jesus say Peter would do before a rooster crowed?

How many times did Peter say he didn't know Jesus?

Did Peter make a good choice or a bad choice?

How did Peter feel when the rooster crowed?

How did Jesus feel?

Think about YOUR Choices

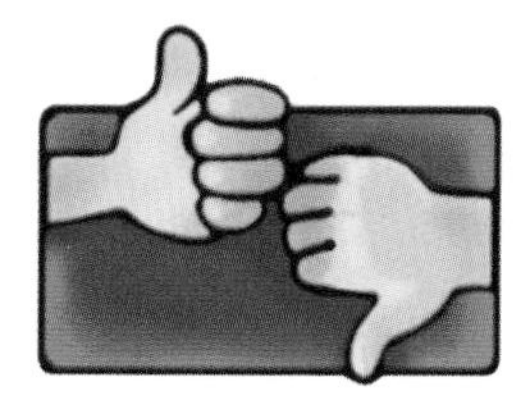

What might you do if someone made fun of you for being Jesus' friend? Would you ask Jesus to help you tell the truth?

Do a Good-Choice Activity

In the dark, turn on a flashlight and wiggle your fingers in front of the light. It looks like a flickering fire. Let that "fire" remind you not to do what Peter did.

We should never be afraid to let people know that we're Jesus' friend.

Pray Together

Dear God, thank you for loving us no matter what we do. But help us to be brave and not be afraid to say we are Jesus' friend. In Jesus' name. Amen.

"He Was God's Son!"

Matthew 27:22-66; Luke 23:44-49; John 19:1-30

CHOICE: Does a Roman soldier believe that Jesus is God's Son? Or does he believe that Jesus isn't anyone special?

Jesus had done nothing wrong. But a Roman ruler listened as the crowd yelled, "Crucify him!"

The people didn't believe that Jesus was God's Son. So they wanted him put on a cross, where he would die. The ruler could see that there would be trouble if he let Jesus go free. So he turned Jesus over to his Roman soldiers.

The soldiers were unkind to Jesus. They made fun of

him and hurt him. Then they put a crown of thorns on his head. And they led him to a hill near the city. They put him on a cross made from two pieces of wood.

Jesus let the soldiers do these things. He knew that it was God's plan for him to die on the cross. He would take the blame for all the wrong things people do.

People kept making fun of Jesus. They called him "King of the Jews." The Roman soldiers played a game to see who would get Jesus' robe.

Jesus' mother, Mary, and some other women stood near the cross. John, one of Jesus' helpers, was with them. They were so sad to see Jesus on the cross.

Then the sky grew dark, even though it was the middle of the day. Jesus felt all alone and called for God. He was tired and thirsty.

By the middle of the afternoon Jesus cried out, "It is finished!" Then he was dead.

Suddenly the earth began to shake, and everyone was afraid.

The Roman soldier who was in charge had watched Jesus all day. He didn't know who Jesus was. But he could tell that strange things were happening.

Now the Roman soldier had a big choice to make. He could believe that Jesus was really God's Son. And he could let everyone know what he believed. Or he could be quiet and forget about what happened. It was getting late. Maybe he could try to figure everything out another day.

What did the soldier in charge do? He looked up to the cross and said, "This man Jesus really was the Son of God!"

A kind man named Joseph of Arimathea took Jesus' body and put it in a little cave in a garden. He rolled a stone in front of the opening to this garden tomb. Then soldiers came to guard the tomb. The leaders sent them so no one could take Jesus' body away.

The soldier who had been in charge at the cross must have felt very sad about what had happened. God was sad about all that had happened too. But God knew that Jesus was not going to stay in the tomb! And God knew what the soldier believed. He believed in God's Son. God was glad that the soldier had said what he believed.

Remember Together

Why did the people want Jesus to be put on a cross to die?

What strange things happened in the middle of the day?

What did the Roman soldier who was in charge say about Jesus?

Did the Roman soldier make a good choice or a bad choice?

Think about YOUR Choices

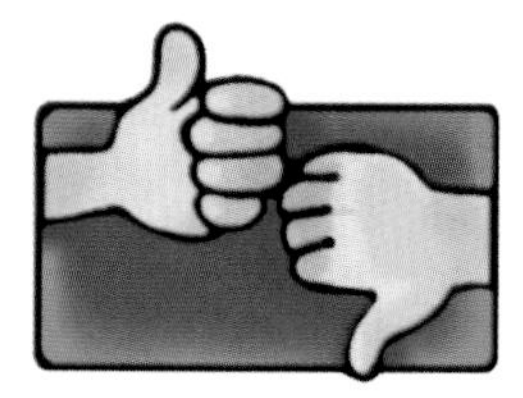

God wants everyone to believe in his Son, Jesus. How did you find out that Jesus is God's Son? Do you believe that Jesus died for you?

Do a Good-Choice Activity

Draw a picture showing the people who were at the cross. Draw simple faces to show how they felt. Then add yourself to your picture. Show how you feel, and tell someone what you might have said to Jesus that day.

Choosing to believe that Jesus is God's Son is the best choice we'll ever make.

Pray Together

Dear God, thank you that we can believe in Jesus, your Son. In his name. Amen.

Early in the Morning

Matthew 28:1-10; Luke 24:9-10

CHOICE: Do Mary and her friends tell the disciples about the angels? Or do they just go home?

How sad Jesus' helpers, the disciples, were. It was early on Sunday morning. It seemed like a long time since Thursday evening. That's when they had eaten dinner with Jesus. They knew they had run away when he needed them most. And on Friday Jesus had died on a cross. Now his disciples were lonely and afraid.

Early on that same Sunday morning, one of Jesus' friends, named Mary, woke up. She dressed quickly and gathered her basket of spices. Tiptoeing, she left her house while it was still dark. She met some other women, and together they walked out of the city of

Jerusalem. They were going back to the garden tomb to put spices on Jesus' body.

As they came near the tomb, they wondered how they would roll away the big stone in front of it. But they didn't have to wonder very long.

Suddenly the earth began to shake. With a loud noise,

an angel appeared and rolled the stone back. Then he sat on it. The guards were so afraid that they fell down. They lay on the ground looking as if they were dead.

Mary and her friends were afraid too. But the angel said, "Don't be afraid. I know you are looking for Jesus. The last time you saw him he was dead. But now he is alive again, just as he said he would be. Come and see for yourselves that he is no longer here.

Then run quickly and tell the disciples that Jesus is alive. Tell them to go to Galilee and see Jesus there."

Mary and her friends started to run, but then they stopped. Would anyone believe them?

Now the women had a big choice to make. They could tell Jesus' helpers what the angel had said. The women could tell them that Jesus was alive. They could tell the men that they could see him in Galilee. Or the women could just quietly go home. Maybe the disciples wouldn't believe them anyway.

What did the women do? They stopped only for a moment, but in that moment Jesus himself appeared to them! He said, "Don't be afraid. Go and tell the others to meet me in Galilee."

Now the women ran as fast as their legs would carry them. They told Peter and all the other disciples that it was all true! Jesus was alive! And they could see him in Galilee.

God rejoiced because his Son, Jesus, was alive again. He rejoiced with the women who saw the empty tomb. And he rejoiced with Jesus' helpers, who learned about the happy news from the women.

Remember Together

When did the women go to the garden?
What did the angel tell the women to do?
Did the women make a good choice or a bad choice?
What did the women say to Jesus' helpers?

Think about YOUR Choices

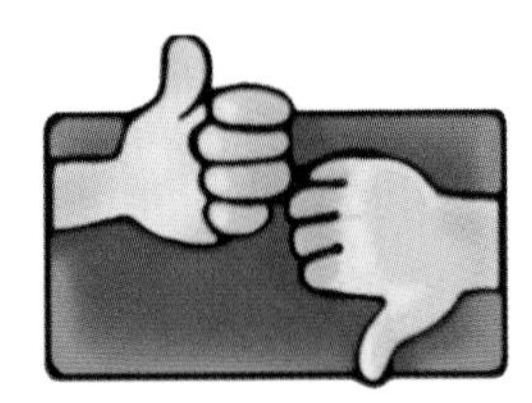

Have you ever heard news that was so good you hardly dared to believe it was true? Did you tell the news to anyone? The news about Jesus coming back to life is the best news of all! Would you like to tell someone about it?

Do a Good-Choice Activity

Choose to get up early some morning and praise God in the first light of day. If it's warm outside, you and your family could go outdoors for a morning song and prayer.

The best news we can share is the news that Jesus is alive.

Pray Together

Dear God, Jesus is alive! Hooray! We're so happy that we've heard the news. And we want everyone else to hear it too. We pray in Jesus' name. Amen.

"I Must See"

John 20:19-31

CHOICE: Does Thomas believe his friends when they say that Jesus is alive? Or does he have to see Jesus for himself?

Could Jesus really be alive again? Jesus wanted his disciples to know that it was true. So he went to them the very first Sunday evening after he came back to life.

The disciples were together in a little room with the doors locked. They were still afraid of the leaders who had put Jesus on the cross. Suddenly, Jesus was standing with them, even though no one had opened the door! He said, "Peace be with you."

How happy Jesus' helpers were to see Jesus again! It really was true. Yes. Jesus was alive! One disciple was not in the little room when Jesus came. His name was Thomas. Later, the other disciples saw Thomas and told him the good news. They said, "We have seen Jesus!" They told Thomas how Jesus had been right there with them. They told him what Jesus had said.

Now Thomas had a big choice to make. He could believe the other disciples and be glad that Jesus was alive. Or he could say that he didn't believe the good news. After all, it was hard for him to believe because he hadn't seen Jesus for himself.

This is what Thomas did. He said, "I won't believe it's true unless I see Jesus myself."

A week later the disciples were in the little room again. This time Thomas was there. Once again the doors were locked. And once again Jesus was suddenly standing with them, even though no one had opened the door.

Jesus said, "Peace be with you." Jesus called Thomas over and invited him not only to see him but to touch him. Then Thomas believed it was true. Jesus really was alive.

God was sorry that Thomas had not believed that Jesus was alive until he saw Jesus. But God loved Thomas and was glad that he finally did believe.

Remember Together

Who was not with the disciples the first time Jesus came?

Why was it hard for Thomas to believe that Jesus was alive?

Did Thomas make a good choice or a bad choice?

How did Jesus help Thomas to believe?

Think about YOUR Choices

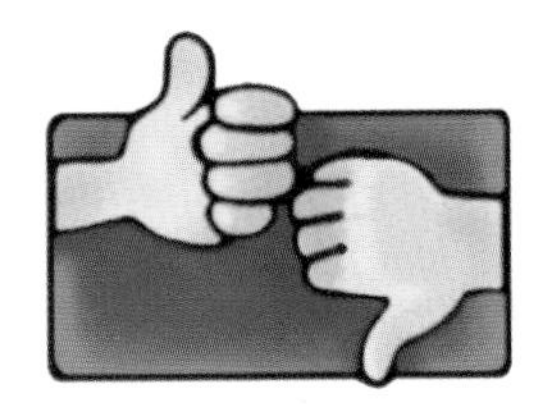

No one can see Jesus today, so what can help you believe that he is alive? (Bible stories, prayer, faith)

Do a Good-Choice Activity

Stand by an open window and describe the wind. Is it a windy day or a calm day? Can you see the wind? How do you know it's there? Pretend you don't believe there is such a thing as wind. Ask a family member to help you believe in it. Then take turns helping each other believe that Jesus is alive.

God is pleased when we believe that his Son, Jesus, is alive.

Pray Together

Dear God, we're glad that your Word tells us Jesus is alive. Thank you for helping us believe. In Jesus' name. Amen.

"Feed My Sheep"

John 21:1-17

CHOICE: Does Peter tell Jesus that he loves him? Or doesn't Peter say anything?

After Jesus came back to life again, his disciples weren't sure what to do. One day Peter said to some of the other disciples, "I'm going fishing." The others said that they would go with Peter. They would go back to their old jobs as fishermen. So they got out their old boats and their old nets. Then they rowed out into the water. Soon they were fishing like they always used to do.

The best time for fishing was at night. But that night the disciples didn't catch even one fish.

Early the next morning they saw someone on the beach. They thought he was a stranger. The man called to them, "Haven't you caught any fish yet?"

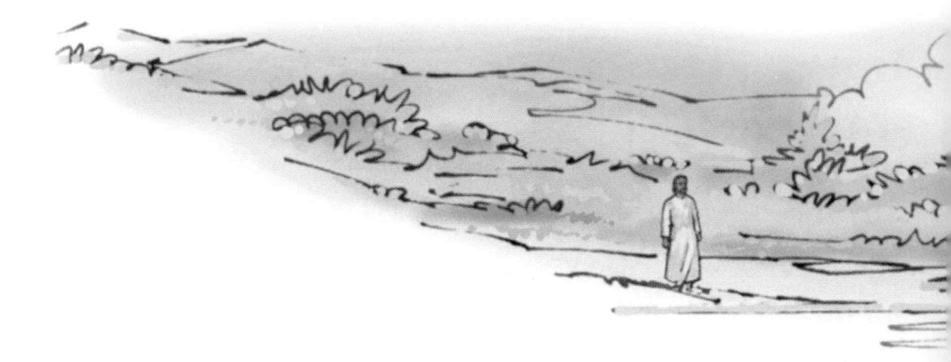

The fishermen called back, “No! Not any.”

The man on the beach called out, “Throw your net into the water again. Put it in the water on the right side of your boat. Then you’ll get some fish.”

The disciples did that. And the net got so full of fish that they couldn’t bring it in. Then John said to Peter, “It’s Jesus!”

Peter looked up. It really was Jesus! Peter was so happy that he jumped out of the boat and swam all the way to shore. The other disciples came behind him in the boat.

Jesus saw Peter swimming toward him. Jesus

remembered the night when Peter said three times that he didn't know Jesus. Now Jesus wanted to let Peter tell him three times that he loved him.

So after giving Peter and the others breakfast on the beach, Jesus talked to Peter. He asked Peter a question, and he asked it three times.

"Peter, do you love me?" asked Jesus.

Now Peter had a big choice to make. He could let

Jesus know how much he loved him. He could say it in front of his friends. Or Peter could say nothing. Perhaps Jesus wouldn't believe him anyway. Had Jesus really forgiven Peter for pretending not to know him?

This is how Peter answered. He said, "Yes, Lord, you know I love you."

Jesus said, "Feed my little sheep." The sheep Jesus was talking about were really people. Jesus was saying that he wanted Peter to keep on telling others about God's love.

Jesus asked a second time, "Peter, do you love me?"

Again Peter answered, "Yes, Lord, you know I love you."

And again Jesus said, "Feed my sheep."

Jesus asked Peter a third time, "Do you really love me?"

Peter said, "Lord, you know everything. You know I love you."

And a third time Jesus answered, "Feed my sheep."

What a happy day it was for Peter on the beach! He knew that Jesus loved him and that Jesus wanted *his* love too. Jesus even wanted Peter to keep on being his helper.

Remember Together

How did Jesus help the disciples with their fishing?
Who swam to shore?
What did Jesus ask Peter?
What was Peter's answer?
Did Peter make a good choice or a bad choice?

Think about YOUR Choices

Has someone ever forgiven you for something you felt really bad about doing? How did it feel to know that this person still loved you? When you do wrong things, does Jesus still love you? Do you tell him that you love him?

Do a Good-Choice Activity

Let Jesus know you love him by singing a song for him. You might want to make up a new song. For example, you could sing "Jesus, I love you. You know I really do." If you like, sing it to the chorus of "Jesus Loves Me."

If we love Jesus, we should tell him so!

Pray Together

Thank you, Jesus, for your love. You know all about me just like you knew all about Peter. And you love me just like you loved Peter. I love you too! Amen.

Everyone Can Understand!

Matthew 28:16-20; Acts 1–2

CHOICE: Has Peter become brave enough to preach about Jesus to a big crowd? Or does he wait for someone else to do it?

It was time for Jesus to go back to God in heaven again. Before Jesus left, he promised that he would still be with his followers forever. Then Jesus said, "Wait here, and God will send his Holy Spirit. He will make you brave and help you tell people everywhere about me."

Jesus went right up into the clouds, and the disciples could no longer see him. Then they waited in the city of Jerusalem for God's Holy Spirit. The people who loved Jesus met together and prayed.

Finally one morning they heard the sound of a loud wind rushing all around them. Something that looked like fire came down on each of them, but it didn't burn them. When they began to talk, they could speak all different languages! Many people from many different places were in the city that day. And all of them could understand Jesus' helpers.

Peter looked at the big crowd of people. What a wonderful time to let a lot of people know about Jesus!

Now Peter had a big choice to make. He could be brave and preach to all these people. Jesus had told Peter to let people know about him. So Peter knew it would be the right thing to do. Or Peter could pretend he didn't know anything about Jesus, as he had done before. He could wait for someone else to preach.

What did Peter do? He spoke loudly to the big crowd, and he was not afraid. God's Holy Spirit made him brave and gave him the right words.

Peter told the people all about Jesus' life. Then he told how Jesus died and came back to life again. Peter said, "Be sorry for all the wrong things you do. Jesus will forgive your sins." About three thousand people believed what Peter said about Jesus!

God was happy that Peter was brave. God was pleased that Peter preached about Jesus.

Remember Together

Before Jesus went to heaven, what did he tell his disciples to do?
After the Holy Spirit came, what did Peter do?
Did Peter make a good choice or a bad choice?

Think about YOUR Choices

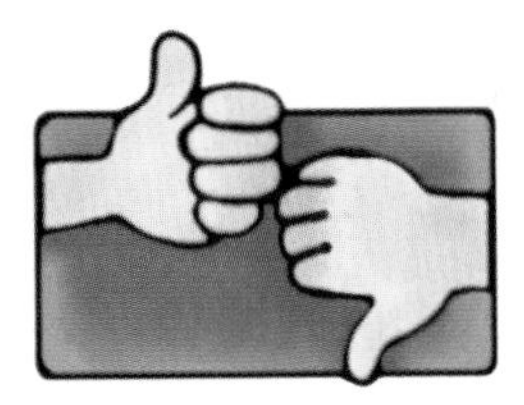

Can you name some people who teach you about Jesus? Who are some people *you* might be able to teach about Jesus? Who will give you the words to say?

Do a Good-Choice Activity

Make a pretty picture for someone by printing these words in big letters: JESUS LOVES YOU! Do you want to make each letter a different color? Perhaps you can print those words in another language, too. Give the picture to someone who understands that language.

We should tell other people that Jesus loves them.

Pray Together

Dear God, we pray for the right words to tell others about Jesus' love. In Jesus' name. Amen.

On the Road

Acts 9:1-22

CHOICE: Does Paul stop doing what's wrong? Or does he keep on doing wrong things?

Paul was a leader who knew God's laws. But he didn't know Jesus. Paul had heard about Jesus. But he didn't believe that Jesus was God's Son. So Paul thought it was wrong to love Jesus.

Paul gave himself the job of finding people who loved Jesus. When he found them, he put them in jail. He believed that what he was doing was the right thing.

One day Paul was on his way to Damascus. He was going there to find more people who loved Jesus. He would have them put in jail. Suddenly, a bright light flashed in the sky. Paul fell down. Then he heard a voice say, "Paul, why are you hurting me?"

Paul asked, "Who are you?"

"I am Jesus. I am the one you are hurting." Jesus had gone to heaven, and he really was God's Son. He wanted Paul to know that. When Paul hurt people who loved Jesus, he was hurting Jesus, too. That was something Jesus also wanted Paul to know.

When Paul tried to get up, he found that he couldn't see anything. So the men who were with him took him by the hand. They led him into Damascus.

For three days Paul stayed at a house on Straight Street. He couldn't see anything. He could pray, however, and he did!

Then a man who loved Jesus came to the house where Paul was. The man said, "Jesus has sent me to

help you see again." Then the man put his hands on Paul. Right away, Paul could see.

Now Paul had a big choice to make. He could believe that Jesus was God's Son. He could believe that it was wrong to put Jesus' friends in jail. And he could stop doing what was wrong. Or Paul could keep believing that Jesus was not God's Son. And he could keep putting Jesus' friends in jail.

What did Paul do? He decided to become one of Jesus' helpers! He talked with Jesus' friends in Damascus for several days. And he began to preach that Jesus is God's Son.

People were very surprised to see how Paul had changed. Paul was no longer putting Jesus' friends in jail. He was teaching more people to believe in Jesus and love him! God was glad that Paul had stopped doing wrong things. And Paul was glad that he finally knew who Jesus really was.

Remember Together

What did Paul do to people who loved Jesus?
Whose voice was in the bright light?
What happened to Paul's eyes?
Did Paul make a good choice or a bad choice?
What did Paul spend the rest of his life doing?

Think about YOUR Choices

Have you ever changed your mind about someone? What helped you change your mind? Did you learn to know the person better? How can you learn to know Jesus better?

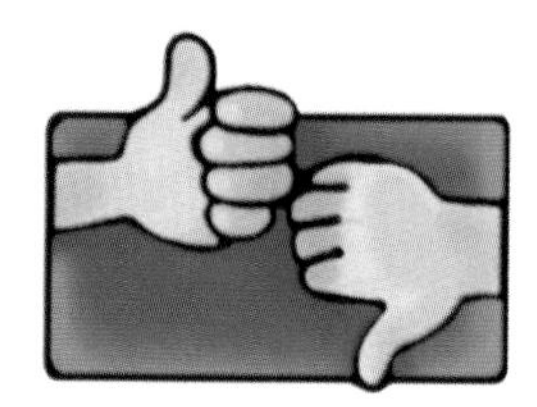

Do a Good-Choice Activity

Cover your eyes and pretend to be Paul. Have someone lead you to a place where you can sit for a while. Then ask Jesus to help you "see" some of the wrong things you've been doing. Ask him to help you stop doing those things.

We show we love Jesus when we stop doing wrong things.

Pray Together

Dear God, thank you for helping us know right from wrong. Teach us to do what's right. In Jesus' name. Amen.

A Warm Welcome

Acts 16:6-15

CHOICE: Does Lydia help God's workers? Or is she too busy?

After Paul learned who Jesus was, he traveled all over the world. He wanted everyone to know about Jesus.

One night Paul had a special dream. He saw a man who lived in Greece. The man asked Paul to please come and help the people there. So the next day Paul got on a boat and left for Greece. His friends Silas, Timothy, and Luke went with him. They sailed for a day. Then they walked to a big city.

One day they walked along a river near the city. They were hoping to find some people by the river. It was God's special day, and they wanted to pray with God's people.

Some women were sitting near the river, so Paul

and his friends sat down with them. Paul told them about Jesus. He told them that God's Son, Jesus, loved them very much.

One woman was named Lydia. She had her own business, selling purple cloth to people. Lydia knew God and prayed to him. But she didn't know Jesus. As Paul talked, God helped her believe Paul's words. She knew now that Jesus was God's Son.

Lydia asked to be baptized. This would let everyone know that she believed in Jesus. Soon everyone at Lydia's house was baptized!

Now Lydia had a big choice to make. She could let God's workers stay at her house. Then she could hear more about Jesus and his love for her. Other people in the city could hear more about Jesus too. Or Lydia could say good-bye to Paul and his friends. She could let them know how busy she was with her business.

What did Lydia do? She invited Paul to stay at her home. Many other people learned about Jesus because of Lydia.

God was glad that Lydia welcomed his helpers. When she did that, Lydia became God's helper too. And that made Lydia feel very good.

Remember Together

Why did Paul and his friends walk along a river?

Who were the people they found by the river?

What did Lydia learn from Paul?

How did Lydia become God's helper?

Did Lydia make a good choice or a bad choice?

Think about YOUR Choices

Sometimes kids, as well as grown-ups, get too busy to do what God wants them to do. What are some things that keep you busy? What things do you want to be sure you're not too busy to do?

Do a Good-Choice Activity

Make a picture chart or a word chart. Show things that you'll make time to do every day. Also show what you'll try to do if you have extra time.

It's always right to find time to be Jesus' helpers.

Pray Together

Dear God, help us to never be too busy to help you. We love you. In Jesus' name. Amen.

Singing in Jail

Acts 16:16-36

CHOICE: Does Paul trust God when it's hard to do? Or does he trust God only when it's easy?

Many people liked the things Paul said. And they learned to believe in Jesus. But some people couldn't understand Jesus' love. They wanted to be powerful and rich instead. Paul's talk about Jesus upset them.

One day some men grabbed Paul and his friend Silas. They had the two men put in jail. Why? So Paul and Silas couldn't teach people about Jesus.

Jail was not a fun place for Paul and Silas to be. The

man in charge of the jail made sure they couldn't get out. Bars on the windows and doors kept them from leaving. Boards with holes in them held their feet and kept them from moving. They had to just sit on the dirt floor of the dark jail room.

Now Paul and Silas had a big choice to make. They could be happy because God was with them even in jail. They could trust God to take care of them. Or they could be sad and cry. They could try on their own to find a way to get out of there. But then they might get hurt.

What did Paul and Silas do? They trusted God. And they didn't act sad at all. In the middle of the night they talked to God. They sang songs to God in the middle of the night too! Everyone in the jail listened to them. They learned a lot about God's love as they listened.

Then the earth began to shake. It shook so hard that the jail doors opened! And the chains came off all the people in jail! The man in charge of the jail was afraid. But Paul shouted, "It's OK! We're all still here."

Then the jailer wanted to learn how to be saved from his sins. He knew that Paul and Silas had been

praying and singing to God. He knew that they could teach him about God. They told him, "Believe in Jesus, and you'll be saved."

The man from the jail did believe! Then he asked Paul and Silas to come home with him. They told his family about Jesus. And everyone believed in him.

The man gave Paul and Silas food to eat. The next morning he told them, "You're free to leave now."

God was pleased that Paul and Silas had trusted him. Paul and Silas were glad that they had stayed faithful to Jesus while they were in jail. They had learned that they could be joyful even during very hard times. It had turned out to be a great night!

Remember Together

Why were Paul and Silas put in jail?
Did they act happy or sad in jail?
Did Paul and Silas make a good choice or a bad choice?
How did they help the man in charge of the jail?

Think about YOUR Choices

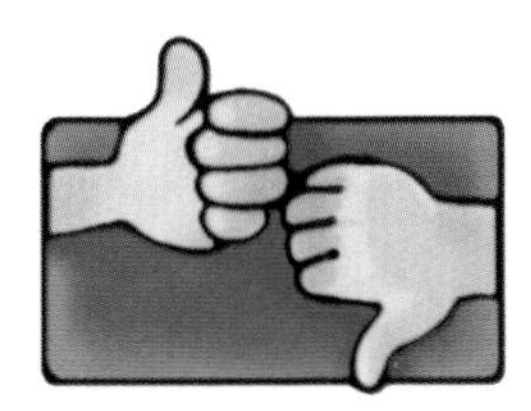

Was there a time when things didn't seem to be going right for you? How might praying and singing and trusting God make a hard time seem easier? What can you choose to do the next time you're upset about something?

Do a Good-Choice Activity

Plan what you can do the next time your family is stuck in traffic or trapped somewhere during a storm. You can memorize songs to sing or Bible verses to say.

We should choose to trust God when we're having a hard time.

Pray Together

Dear God, thanks for being with us through hard times. Help us to always keep trusting you. In Jesus' name. Amen.

Learning All about Jesus

Acts 18

CHOICE: Does Apollos listen to his teachers? Or does he think he doesn't need to learn about Jesus?

After Paul got out of jail, he started traveling again. He walked from town to town, telling people about Jesus.

One day Paul came to a city where he made some new friends. His new friends were a husband and wife named Aquila and Priscilla. Paul lived with them and worked with them. All three of them made tents.

Every week on God's special day, Paul went to the synagogue. That was the place where people went to worship God. The people there loved God. But they didn't know about his Son, Jesus. Some of the people didn't believe what Paul told them about Jesus. But other people believed in Jesus and learned to love him.

Then Paul moved into another house. He stayed there for over a year. He spent all his time teaching people about Jesus.

Finally it was time for Paul to get on a boat. God wanted him to go to another town and teach more people about Jesus.

Paul took his friends Aquila and Priscilla with him. When they came to another town, Paul stayed for a while. But then he traveled to still more towns. This time Aquila and Priscilla didn't go with him.

On God's special day Aquila and his wife, Priscilla,

went to a synagogue. It was in the town where they were living now. At this special place to worship God, they heard a man preach. The man's name was Apollos, and he was a good teacher. But Paul's friends could tell that he didn't know about Jesus.

When Apollos was done preaching, Aquila and Priscilla asked if they could talk to him. Then they began telling him everything they had learned from Paul about Jesus.

Now Apollos had a big choice to make. He could listen to this man and woman. He could let them teach him all about Jesus. Then he could start teaching other people about Jesus too. Or he could tell Aquila and Priscilla that he didn't want to listen to them. He could say that he knew all he needed to know about God.

What did Apollos do? He listened to everything Aquila and Priscilla said. Apollos learned all about Jesus. Then he traveled to another town and talked to the people there about Jesus. He helped the people understand who Jesus was. He said, "You are waiting for God to send someone to you. God has already sent Jesus! He is God's Son. Jesus is the one you are looking for." Many people learned about Jesus because of Apollos.

God was glad that Apollos listened to Aquila and Priscilla. They were good teachers, and Apollos was a good listener. He learned all about God's Son, Jesus. Then he became a good teacher too!

Remember Together

What did Paul and his two new friends make?

Who went with Paul when he sailed to another town?

Who did Aquila and Priscilla want to teach Apollos about?

Did Apollos make a good choice or a bad choice?

Then who did Apollos teach other people about?

Think about YOUR Choices

What have you already learned about Jesus? Do you want to keep learning more about him? Remember that Apollos was a grown-up, but he still needed to learn about Jesus!

Do a Good-Choice Activity

Choose a favorite story about Jesus. Try to learn something new from that story. Then practice telling it to your dolls or stuffed animals. When you know the story really well, tell it to another person.

Wanting to learn more about Jesus is a very good choice to make!

Pray Together

Dear God, thank you for Bible stories that teach us about Jesus. Thank you for teachers who help us learn what the Bible says. In Jesus' name. Amen.

Index to Some Bible People Who Made Choices

Old Testament

New Testament

Passing On the Truth to Our Next Generation

The Right From Wrong message, available in numerous formats, provides a blueprint for countering the culture and rebuilding the crumbling foundations of our families.

The Right From Wrong Book for Adults

Right From Wrong: What You Need to Know to Help Youth Make Right Choices
by Josh McDowell and Bob Hostetler

Our youth no longer live in a culture that teaches an objective standard of right and wrong. Truth has become a matter of taste. Morality has been replaced by individual preference. And today's youth have been affected. Fifty-seven percent of our churched youth cannot state that an objective standard of right and wrong even exists!

As the centerpiece of the Right From Wrong Campaign, this life-changing book provides you with a biblical, yet practical, blueprint for passing on core Christian values to the next generation.

Right From Wrong, Trade Paper Book
ISBN 0-8499-3604-7

Truth Slayers, Trade Paper Book
ISBN 0-8499-3662-4

The Truth Slayers Book for Youth

Truth Slayers: The Battle of Right From Wrong
by Josh McDowell and Bob Hostetler

This book, directed to youth, is written in the popular NovelPlus format. It combines the fascinating story of Brittney Marsh, Philip Milford, Jason Withers, and the consequences of their wrong choices with Josh McDowell's insights for young adults in sections called "The Inside Story."

Truth Slayers conveys the critical Right From Wrong message that challenges you to rely on God's Word as the absolute standard of truth in making right choices.

103 Questions Book for Children

103 Questions Children Ask about Right From Wrong
Introduction by Josh McDowell

"How does a person really know what is right or wrong?" "How does God decide what's wrong?" "If lying is wrong, why did God let some people in the Bible tell lies?" "What is a conscience and where does it come from?" These and 99 other questions are what kids ages 6 to 10 are asking. The *103 Questions* book equips parents to answer the tough questions kids ask about right from wrong. It also provides an easy-to-understand book that children will read and enjoy.

103 Questions, Trade Paper Book
ISBN 0-8423-4595-7

Workbook for Junior High and High School Students

Setting You Free to Make Right Choices
Workbook and Leader's Guide
by Josh McDowell

With a Bible-based emphasis, this workbook creatively and systematically teaches your students how to determine right from wrong in their everyday lives—specifically applying the decision-making process to moral questions about lying, cheating, getting even, and premarital sex.

Through eight youth group meetings, followed each week by five daily exercises of 20 to 25 minutes per day, your teenagers will be challenged to develop a lifelong habit of making right moral choices.

Setting You Free to Make Right Choices,
Member's Workbook ISBN 0-8054-9828-1
Setting You Free to Make Right Choices,
Leader's Guide ISBN 0-8054-9829-X

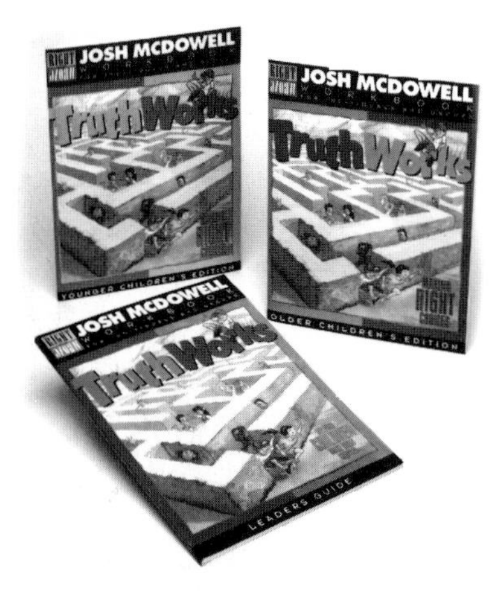

Workbooks for Children

Truth Works: Making Right Choices
Workbooks and Leader's Guide
by Josh McDowell

To pass on the truth and reclaim a generation, we must teach God's truth when our children's minds and hearts are young and pliable. Creatively developed, *Truth Works* includes two workbooks, one directed to younger children in grades one to three, the other to older children in grades four to six.

In eight fun-filled group sessions, your children will discover why such truths as honesty, justice, love, purity, self-control, mercy, and respect work to their best interests. They will see how four simple steps will help them to make right moral choices an everyday habit.

Truth Works, Younger Children's Workbook ISBN 0-8054-9831-1
Truth Works, Older Children's Workbook ISBN 0-8054-9830-3
Truth Works, Leader's Guide ISBN 0-8054-9827-3

Contact your Christian supplier to help you obtain these Right From Wrong resources and begin to make it right in your home, your church, and your community.

CAMPAIGN RIGHT FROM WRONG® RESOURCES

Workbook for Adults

Truth Matters for You and Tomorrow's Generation
Workbook and Leader's Guide
by Josh McDowell

The *Truth Matters* workbook includes 35 daily activities that help you to instill within your children and youth such biblical values as honesty, love, and sexual purity. By taking just 25 to 30 minutes each day, you will discover a fresh and effective way to teach your family how to make right choices—even in tough situations.

The *Truth Matters* workbook is designed to be used in eight adult group sessions that encourage interaction and support building. The five daily activities between each group meeting will help you and your family to make right choices a habit.

Truth Matters,
Member's Workbook
ISBN 0-8054-9834-6
Truth Matters, Leader's Guide
ISBN 0-8054-9833-8

Workbook for College Students

Out of the Moral Maze, Workbook with Leader's Instructions
by Josh McDowell

Students entering college face a culture that has lost its belief in absolutes. In today's society, truth is a matter of taste; morality, a matter of individual preference. *Out of the Moral Maze* will provide any truth-seeking collegiate with a sound moral guidance system based on God and his Word as the determining factors for making right moral choices.

Out of the Moral Maze
Member's Workbook and Leader's Instructions
ISBN 0-8054-9832-X

CAMPAIGN RESOURCES

Truth Matters,
Adult Video Series
ISBN 0-8499-8587-0

Setting Youth Free to Make Right Choices, Youth Video Series
ISBN 0-8499-8585-4

Video Series for Adults and Youth

Truth Matters for You and Tomorrow's Generation Five-part adult video series featuring Josh McDowell
Setting Youth Free to Make Right Choices Five-part youth video series featuring Josh McDowell

These two interactive video series go beyond declaring what is right and wrong. They teach how to make right moral choices based on God's absolute standard of truth.

The adult series includes five video sessions, a comprehensive Leader's Guide with samplers from the five *Right From Wrong* workbooks, the *Right From Wrong* book, the *Truth Slayers* book, and an eight-minute promotional tape that will motivate adults to go through the series.

The youth series contains five video sessions, a Leader's Guide with reproducible handouts that include samplers from the *Right From Wrong* workbooks, and the *Truth Slayers* book.

The Right From Wrong Musicals for Youth

Truth Works musical by Dennis and Nan Allen
Truth Slayers musical by Steven V. Taylor and Matt Tullos

The *Truth Slayers* musical for junior high and high school students is based on the *Truth Slayers* book. The *Truth Works* musical for children is based on the *Truth Works* workbooks. As youth and children perform these musicals for their peers and families, they have a unique opportunity to tell of the life-changing message of Right From Wrong.

Each musical includes complete leader's instructions, a songbook of all music used, a dramatic script, and an accompanying soundtrack on cassette or compact disc.

CAMPAIGN RIGHT FROM WRONG® RESOURCES

The Topsy-Turvy Kingdom Picture Book

The Topsy-Turvy Kingdom
by Dottie and Josh McDowell, with David Weiss

This fascinating story from a faraway land is written in delightful rhyme. It enables adults to teach children the importance of believing in and obeying an absolute standard of truth.

The Topsy-Turvy Kingdom, Hardcover Book for Children
ISBN 0-8423-7218-0

The Josh McDowell Family and Youth Devotionals

Josh McDowell's One Year Book of Youth Devotions by Bob Hostetler
Josh McDowell's One Year Book of Family Devotions by Bob Hostetler

These two devotionals may be used alone or together. Youth from ages 10 through 16 will enjoy the youth devotionals on their own. And they'll be able to participate in the family devotionals with their parents and siblings. Both devotionals are packed with fun-filled and inspiring readings. They will challenge you to think—and live—as "children of God without fault in a crooked and depraved generation, in which you shine like stars in the universe" (Philippians 2:15, NIV).

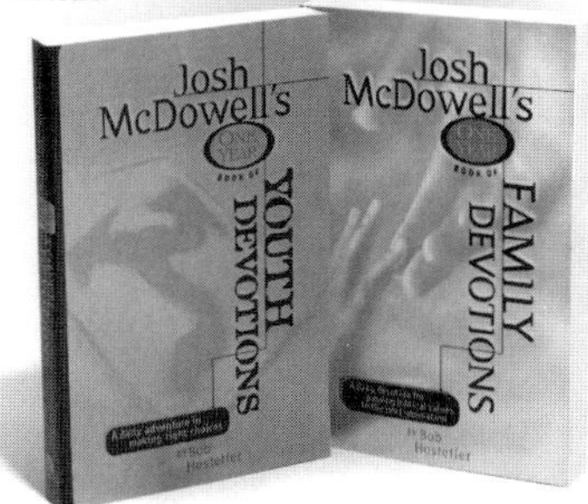

Josh McDowell's One Year Book of Youth Devotions
ISBN 0-8423-4301-6
Josh McDowell's One Year Book of Family Devotions
ISBN 0-8423-4302-4

Josh and Dottie McDowell bring the "Right from Wrong" campaign to a child's level in *The Right Choices Bible.*

Josh McDowell, well known for his "Why Wait" and "Right from Wrong" campaigns, is one of today's most articulate and popular speakers. He has spoken to more than seven million young people in at least eighty-four countries on more than seven hundred university and college campuses. He is also the author of over fifty books and has been featured in numerous films, videos, and television specials. In addition, he also hosts his own weekly radio and television programs.

Josh and Dottie, who have been married for twenty-seven years, are the parents of four children. This Bible storybook, which they have coauthored, helps meet the challenge to pass biblical values on to the next generation.